# PRAISE FOR NANCY BOYARSKY'S NICOLE GRAVES MYSTERIES

"full of page-by-page surprises"
—*Kirkus Reviews*

"...nail-biting adventure whose thralls are difficult to escape"
—*Foreword Reviews*

"a hold-onto-the-bar roller coaster of a mystery"
—*RT Book Reviews*

"Nicole Graves is the best fictional sleuth to come down the pike since Sue Grafton's Kinsey Millhone."
—Laura Levine, author of the popular *Jaine Austen Mysteries*

"a charming and straight-shooting heroine"
—*Foreword Reviews*

"Well written, non-stop, can't-put-it-down suspense."
—Charles Rosenberg, bestselling author of *Death on a High Floor*

"Well developed characters in a rich English setting brings ample twists throughout and all the way to the final pages."

—Eric Hoffer Award Gold Winner 2018 for *The Swap*

# THE RANSOM

*a Nicole Graves mystery*

## NANCY BOYARSKY

**Light Messages**

Durham, NC

Published 2019, by Light Messages
www.lightmessages.com
Durham, NC 27713 USA
SAN: 920-9298

Paperback ISBN: 978-1-61153-317-0
Ebook ISBN: 978-1-61153-318-7
Library of Congress Control Number: 2019939448

*For my wonderful and amazing daughter Jennifer*

# ONE

NICOLE GRAVES ARRIVED AT WORK to find a manila envelope on her desk. It bore a yellow sticky note from her boss:

> Take a look at this. Then come
>
> to my office and I'll explain.
>
> —Jerry

She pulled out the contents of the envelope. First was a news article she'd seen in the paper several days ago. It described the home invasion of a wealthy couple in which the wife was kidnapped. This was the third such incident in as many months. Nicole had read about the crimes and found them intriguing, especially since kidnapping of adults for ransom was rare in Los Angeles and other American cities.

In the first case, the husband, whose name was never disclosed in the news, followed the abductors' instructions to the letter. They'd warned him not to call the police, and he didn't. He delivered fifty thousand dollars ransom in cash—unmarked bills of assorted denominations—as demanded. The drop point was L.A.'s downtown central library, behind the books on a shelf holding copies of Shakespeare's *All's Well That Ends Well*. Only after his wife was released did the husband report the crime to the police. The tabloids had a field day with the story, referring to the perpetrators as the "All's-Well Kidnappers." It did have a certain ring to it.

In the second case a month later, Craig Reina also followed instructions not to involve the police when his wife, Victoria, was kidnapped. He delivered the ransom to a public park, where he'd been instructed to leave it under a slide set. After twenty-four hours passed with no sign of his wife, Reina finally called the police. Now, six weeks later, Victoria Reina was still missing, and the police didn't seem to have a clue to her whereabouts.

The third case, described in the article Jerry had left, took place five days ago. In this instance, the kidnap victim's husband had been killed, and his wife was still missing. In the previous kidnappings, the wife had been taken while the husband was left drugged, tied up, but otherwise unharmed. The intruders had disguised themselves so well that no one could give a physical description, except that the kidnappers were three in number and probably male. Not only had they covered their faces and worn gloves, none of them had spoken a word during the home invasions.

Nicole was insatiably curious when it came to crimes serious or bizarre enough to make the news. She found two aspects of these incidents intriguing. One was the way most crimes and attempted cover-ups were so badly bungled that the perpetrators had to be stupid, crazy, or both to imagine they'd get away with it.

When Nicole had read about the first two home invasion-kidnapping cases, she'd been puzzled by the relatively modest amount of ransom when the victims were extremely wealthy and probably would have paid a great deal more. Were the guilty parties kids, unaware of how much money to demand? Or was this rash of kidnappings something else altogether, like a sophisticated insurance scam or a weird, twisted prank that was the product of a sick mind?

In the most recent home invasion, which involved Brad and Ashley Rexton, things had gone wrong from the start. Brad Rexton was found dead at the scene, the victim of blunt trauma to the head. It appeared he'd tried to fight off the intruders and had fallen or been knocked down and struck his head against the corner of a marble fireplace. The intruders had disconnected the home's security cameras, approaching them from behind to avoid being caught on video. However, they'd missed one camera hidden in the front shrubbery. It showed three men in hoodies and ski masks carrying Ashley, limp and apparently unconscious, out of the house. They put her in the back of a white van with no visible license plate and got in. The van started up and disappeared from view.

This case stood out from the others in several ways. For one thing, the ransom demand was much bigger. A message, traced to a burner phone with no clue to the identity of its owner, had been left on the couple's voicemail. The caller demanded twenty thousand dollars in cash, less than in the other cases. But this was described as a "good faith" down payment on a whopping $10 million that had to be delivered before Ashley's release. That amount was to be wire-transferred to an offshore account. The kidnapper said he'd be in touch with further instructions after the cash payment was received.

The crime had taken place on a Saturday night. Brad's body, along with the phone message, hadn't been found until Tuesday morning, when the Rexton's housekeeper arrived. That evening, the police held a press conference. The police chief, quoted widely on the news, said, "We're putting all our resources into finding both missing women—Victoria Reina and Ashley Rexton—and apprehending those responsible for the death of Bradley Rexton."

After the crime was reported, the bank discovered that the couple's joint checking account, holding a relatively modest $9,562, had been cleaned out the night of the kidnapping at various ATMs. In addition, a failed attempt had been made to hack Brad Rexton's investment account through the bank's website. As of now, no clue had been found to Ashley's whereabouts.

Nicole knew who the Rextons were. Robert Rexton, the father of the murdered man, was CEO of Rexton Enterprises, Inc., a land development company that happened to be a client of Nicole's employer, Colbert and Smith Investigations. As a newly licensed PI, Nicole had done work for Rexton Enterprises when they were trying to collect a settlement from another business that had hidden its assets. Nicole had found a shell company holding the money, and Rexton had gotten his settlement.

In the envelope with the news clipping were an address book and a daily diary. Each had "Ashley Rexton" stamped in gold on its red-leather cover. Nicole flipped through the pages, noting the neat, feminine handwriting, which she presumed to be Ashley's. The books brought up a question: Why hadn't they been turned over to the police?

More importantly, why had Jerry left this material on Nicole's desk? Surely, he didn't expect her to investigate a murder-kidnapping when law enforcement would be all over it. She was intrigued, of course, but Colbert and Smith never took on cases that were the province of the police. Nor did they look for missing persons, except for the rare occasions when an important client's minor child ran away.

Nicole got up and, with the envelope under her arm, walked down the hall to her boss's office. The door was open. She went in, sat down, and placed the material on Jerry's desk.

"What's this about?" she said.

Jerry leaned back in his chair and put his feet on his desk. "Rexton asked us to look into his daughter-in-law's background. Find out who she was, where she came from, and what she was doing before she walked into his son's life."

Nicole shifted in her seat. "She was married to Brad for over a year. Sounds like she and her father-in-law didn't have much of a relationship."

"You're right about that," Jerry said. "Rexton said he spotted her as a gold digger the moment he laid eyes on her. She never talked about her past, and she clammed up when anyone asked about it."

Nicole held up the envelope. "The address and date books— shouldn't they have been turned over to the police?"

"Rexton gave the police copies. He told them that was all he'd found. For some reason, he wanted to keep the originals. They were left on his yacht; the couple had borrowed it shortly before the home invasion. Rexton says the police weren't interested in Ashley's background. He got the impression they thought it was irrelevant. But he believes Ashley was behind her own kidnapping and responsible for his son's death. Before the wedding, he told his son he was going to have an investigator look into her background. Brad got so angry that Rexton backed off."

Nicole flipped through the pages of the address book. It held a fair number of names. "You want me to contact these people and interview them? You realize, don't you, that the police will get wind of it. They won't like it."

"I agree, but Rexton is one of our biggest clients. I tried to talk him out of it. When he wouldn't see reason, I said I'd put my best investigator on it."

"Gee, thanks," Nicole said. "I'd be flattered if I didn't know it's going to be a waste of time that will rile up the cops." She paused for a moment, staring at the envelope before going on. "What's Rexton thinking? If she's still alive and is being held hostage, wouldn't the kidnappers be trying to shake the ransom out of him? Or if she really was behind the whole thing, wouldn't her husband's death have motivated her to disappear?"

"I knew you'd see the angles," Jerry said.

Nicole gave him an incredulous look. "This is just plain dumb. The police have all kinds of resources we don't. What can we do that they can't?"

"Look," Jerry said. "Rexton's a very important client and always wants results, like, yesterday. He's used to giving orders and having them followed. The police aren't doing his bidding. His reasoning is that if we can track down deadbeats and sift through shell corporations, how much harder can this be? He's given us her contacts, as well as her date book. Start out by calling Rexton. Make an appointment with him and find out what he does know about Ashley. Today's Thursday. See if you can get in later today or tomorrow so you can start the investigation as soon as possible. You'll want to interview the people in her address book and anyone else who might know about her past. Nobody expects you to get involved in the kidnapping case, much less find her. In fact, be careful to stay clear of the police investigation."

As she was heading for the door, Jerry said, "Thanks for being such a good sport about this, Nicole."

She gave him a mock frown. "Don't be ridiculous, Jerry. I'm a terrible sport, and you know it."

They both laughed.

Nicole went back to her office and made the call. Rexton's secretary said he was out of the office for the day but could meet with her at three thirty the next afternoon.

This taken care of, she began going through the date book, comparing it to the address book, making a list of people to contact. She decided not to call anyone until she talked to Rexton. But she'd already made up her mind that the first person she'd get in touch with would be Antonia—no last name given, just the word "housekeeper"—who appeared under A in Ashley's address book. According to the paper, it was Antonia who'd found Brad's body. And, as their housekeeper, she could probably shed some light on the couple's relationship.

When Nicole finished looking through the address and

date books, she went online and did a search for information on Ashley, then turned to one of her company's subscription databases that provided a deeper look at individuals. She was relieved to find only one Ashley Rexton in L.A. This made her job infinitely easier than having to track down someone with a common name, like a Jane Smith or a Robert Jones.

Nicole then used Google to find photos of Ashley. It came up with glamour shots that looked as if they'd been taken by a professional photographer. Ashley was a generic Southern California beauty with long, straight blonde hair parted in the middle, blue eyes, full lips and unrealistically lush eyelashes.

Nicole scrolled the record to a news article announcing Ashley's marriage to Brad Rexton the year before. It included a photo of the couple. She studied it closely, noting Ashley's beauty again. Focusing on Brad, she was struck by the contrast between bride and groom. The bride was as lovely as she had been in her glamour shot, dressed in a designer suit and a little hat with a veil. She was beaming broadly.

The groom was more restrained, smiling self-consciously. He was seriously overweight, dressed in—given his proportions— what had to be a custom-tailored suit. He wore no tie, and his shirt was open at the neck, giving the impression that he didn't much care about his appearance. His dark hair had been gelled and combed straight back. His heavy eyebrows slanted downward, and he sported an unkempt mustache and beard. At least in terms of appearance, he and his bride were an odd match.

The database said Ashley was twenty-eight and showed she was a licensed medical assistant. A partial social security number was given, not unusual for a database report, but not enough for Nicole to check it out. There was no record of arrests or convictions. Scrolling through Ashley's record, Nicole found it went back only six years. At that time, she was listed on a website as a staff member of an orthopedic clinic in Albuquerque. But records showed she'd left Albuquerque for Miami in the middle of that year. She'd changed cities several times since: from Miami to Vail. Next was a move to San Francisco, on to Seattle, and finally to Los Angeles. She'd rented an apartment in L.A. only a month before meeting Brad Rexton. Other than that, there was little to go on. The records showed no credit rating, education, place of birth, or relatives.

Ashley's report was unusual in being so incomplete. Her frequent moves weren't that odd for a young person not quite settled in her profession. One thing did strike Nicole as strange—the absence of known relatives. Maybe Ashley had been a runaway in her teens or an orphan, aged out of foster care. But, as Nicole knew, it was hard to draw conclusions with so little information. One possibility was that she was born to U.S. citizens abroad and, except for the stint in the orthopedic clinic, had no employment records in this country. If she'd lived abroad, that would explain the missing place of birth and relatives.

Perhaps Ashley Knowles wasn't her real name. Nicole could think of a lot of reasons why someone might use an assumed name. Maybe she was a con artist who was after her husband's money, as her father-in-law suspected. But there were other possibilities. She might have a past she wanted to hide, perhaps trouble with the law. She might have creditors looking for her. She could be hiding from a stalker or a difficult family situation. Maybe she'd won the lottery and wanted to insulate herself from begging relatives. She probably wasn't in the witness protection program, since they would have provided her with a credible past. Still, there were a lot of legitimate reasons why Ashley might change her name. Of course, there were illegitimate ones, as well.

§

The next afternoon, Nicole drove out to Rexton Enterprises in Santa Monica. It occupied the top floor of a distinctive white office building overlooking the bay. Each floor was recessed from the one below, giving the exterior a stair-step effect. Inside, the lobby was minimalist in décor so that the front wall of windows, with its view of the beach and water, provided the focal point. Blond, parquet floors were polished to a high gloss.

In the elevator, Nicole turned off her phone so her interview of Rexton wouldn't be interrupted. She introduced herself to the front-desk receptionist and was directed down a long corridor, where a secretary was stationed next to a pair of wide double doors.

"You must be Nicole Graves," the secretary said. "He's expecting you." She got up and knocked on one of the doors. If there was a response from inside, Nicole didn't hear it.

"Go right in," the secretary said.

Nicole was ushered into an enormous office that at first appeared empty. As in the lobby, floor-to-ceiling windows faced west, and the afternoon sun was almost blinding. As her sight adjusted, she looked around and, still seeing no one, fixed her eyes on a gold statue standing on a mahogany table in the center of the room. The statue was a stunning copy of *Winged Victory*, except that this version was no more than three-feet high, gilded, and—unlike the original—complete with arms and a head. She was gazing up at a wreath she held aloft.

"Why don't you take a seat over here?" The voice came from Nicole's left. She turned and, for the first time, noticed a man sitting at a desk. He had gray hair and was dressed in a light gray suit and tie, which blended into the subdued tones of the office. Except for *Winged Victory* and a few splotches of color on some abstract paintings, the decor was completely neutral. As in the lobby, the understated décor amplified the bright hues of the beach, water, and sky visible through the big windows.

As Nicole walked over to the desk, she noticed it was completely clean except for a silver-toned telephone with a lot of buttons. Facing the desk, a high-backed chair awaited her.

Without getting up, Rexton reached his hand over his desk, and Nicole leaned in to shake it. "I apologize for not standing," he said, "but, as you can see . . . "

He left the sentence unfinished because, as she bent forward, she saw that he was in a wheelchair. "Have a seat," he said, "and we can get started. Would you like some coffee? Water perhaps?" His voice was deep and commanding. Clearly, he was used to being in charge and had no use for small talk. He didn't smile, nor did he appear bereaved. He betrayed no emotion at all.

"No, I'm fine, thanks. I've prepared some questions." She sat down and pulled a sheet of paper from her purse.

Rexton nodded, indicating she should go ahead.

"Jerry Stevens, my boss, said you were suspicious of Ashley from the start," she said. "Can you tell me why?"

"To put it bluntly," he said, "she wasn't the kind of woman who'd be interested in Bradley. Oh, he was well liked; had a lot of friends—'bros,' he called them. But he'd never had much luck with women, and she was way out of his league. After my son was murdered, I asked my people to look into Ashley's background. They couldn't find much. With all the information available on the Internet, I thought this was strange."

Nicole nodded. "I noticed the same thing. She only goes back six years on our databases, but there could be legitimate reasons for that."

Rexton went on as if he hadn't heard. "I sensed something off about her the first time we met. She was excessively demonstrative toward my son—constantly touching him, reaching out to pat his leg or hold his hand, and—God help me—nuzzling him, nibbling his neck and ears. To me, it looked like an act. Later, when I asked her about herself—family, hometown, schooling—she was evasive. She did say her father was in the service and that she was born in the Philippines where he was stationed at the time. The family moved around a lot while she was growing up. She told me she'd completed college online at the University of Phoenix. I had someone check with the university, but they had no record of her.

"She was shopping—or pretending to shop—at one of those

luxury stores on Rodeo Drive when my son met her. I think it was Gucci. He was looking for a watch. She struck up a conversation and proceeded to help him pick one. He was crazy about her from the start and took great exception when I asked about her background."

"Why do you think that was?"

He raised an eyebrow. "It's obvious, isn't it? He knew what I was thinking: that he couldn't have attracted such a beautiful woman unless she was after his money. You see, he inherited a goodly sum from his grandmother when he was a child. I placed it in an investment account, and it's nearly tripled. That's what she was after, but she had no way to get at it. The money is in a trust, which I control. He has—had to get my signature before he could dip into it. My policy was to grant his requests, if they were reasonable. He was to gain full control of the money on his thirtieth birthday, which would have been in three years.

Rexton was silent before he went on, perhaps thinking about his son's birthday, which was never going to happen. "I think Ashley imagined I'd sign off on a big withdrawal if she'd been kidnapped and held for ransom. I wouldn't have done it, by the way, but that's a moot point.

"I wish now I'd listened to my instincts and had her investigated in the first place. Now my son is dead, and I could have prevented it." His voice cracked and he took a moment to compose himself. "Do you know what they did to him? They left him mortally wounded, and he bled to death."

Nicole paused and nodded, silently acknowledging Rexton's loss before asking, "You think your daughter-in-law engineered the home invasion and kidnapping to get his money?"

"That's right, but the police aren't buying it. Bradley seemed to be under the delusion that she married him for love. In the last few months, he seemed down whenever I saw him. I could tell he was unhappy. When I asked if there was trouble between him and Ashley, he got mad. He was barely speaking to me in the weeks before his death."

"Can you tell me anything more about Ashley?" Nicole said. "Anything at all. What about family? Friends?"

"She said her parents were dead, and she was an only child. So, no family. Her friends were mainly the girlfriends and wives of Brad's crowd, people she'd met through him. She might have had friends before the marriage, but as far as I know, they never came around. I thought you could go through her address book, call the people listed, and learn more about her."

"What about her interests, hobbies?"

"Shopping. That was her passion. She spent a lot of time in Beverly Hills buying designer clothes. She loved spas and had a daily visit from a personal trainer. She was in some kind of high-roller circle at Neiman Marcus that gave her entry to a VIP dining room. She'd take friends there for lunch. Every month, Brad would come to me asking for fifteen thousand dollars to twenty thousand dollars from his trust. I didn't have to ask why he was short. It was Ashley's constant spending."

"Did Brad have a job?"

"He worked for my company as vice president of public affairs. But it was more title than job. He had very little interest in it and rarely bothered to come in. I paid him a handsome salary, believe me."

Nicole wondered about Rexton's feelings for his son. Bradley's lack of ambition must have been a disappointment. What had been the dynamic between them? Even if they'd had a good relationship, it had fallen apart once Ashley came into the picture.

"Back to Ashley and the way she spent her time," she said. "Did she like to travel? Was there any particular place she liked to visit?"

"Not really. They went to some fancy resort in Cabo for their honeymoon but came back early. I had the feeling Ashley was bored."

"Jerry told me your son and Ashley borrowed your yacht

recently," Nicole said. "Where did they go?"

"To Catalina and the Channel Islands."

"Are they into fishing and deep-sea diving?"

"I doubt it," he said.

"That doesn't leave much to do except look at the scenery. Did they enjoy it?"

"I don't know. As I said, my son and I were barely talking at that point."

Nicole was quiet. She had the feeling this was all she was going to get from Rexton. Perhaps it was all he knew.

She got up and thanked him. As she started for the door, he said, "Wait, I just remembered something." He used his hands to propel his wheelchair to her side.

"As a wedding gift," Rexton said, "I gave them three pieces of art that were worth a good amount of money. One was a Picasso—not an original, but a rare limited edition lithograph. An unusual piece, very nice. A few months after they were married, they invited me for dinner. Ashley had just finished decorating the house. She'd hung a lot of big abstract paintings on the walls—not a Kandinski or a de Kooning—" He paused to gesture at the art on his walls. "Those were cheap knockoffs, the sort of thing you'd pick up at a furniture store. When I left, my son saw me out, and I asked what had happened to the art I'd given them. He said Ashley had used a decorator, and those pieces didn't fit in. I told him that if they were sitting in a closet somewhere, I'd like them back.

"That made Brad bristle. He told me that Ashley had given them to a charity or something. My guess is she sold the pieces. They were easily worth $500,000, if not more. That was when my suspicion really took hold. But Brad was too besotted to believe she was just after his money." He paused and then added, "Or maybe he was in denial. I want you to find out who she was. That's all. If it's relevant to my son's murder, I'll turn the information over to the police."

"Here's my email address," Nicole handed him her card. "If you think of anything else, let me know."

Rexton began wheeling himself toward the door, leading her out. He was expert at maneuvering the wheelchair in a way that said he'd been in one for a long time. Nicole, always curious, wondered how his disability had come about.

"Thank you for taking this on," he said. "I hope you find out where she came from and what she was up to."

He offered his hand again. She shook it, and, after a final glance at *Winged Victory*, left his office. It struck her that the statue must be a symbol to Rexton. Winning gave his life meaning; it was what made him happy, and he'd succeeded spectacularly—until now.

# Two

Nicole spent the weekend unpacking boxes and getting settled in her new home. It was a two-bedroom condo, and she was quite in love with it. The building was only a year old. Her unit had a spacious living room and high-tech kitchen. Best of all, it was located in L.A.'s mid-Wilshire district, a short walk from her office. She'd left the apartment she'd been renting in Westwood. The main reason was that her daily commute, a mere five miles, could take up to forty minutes because of the traffic. Mortgage payments on the new condo were a stretch. But she was due for a raise and pretty sure she could manage.

Monday morning, as she was on her way to the office, her cell phone rang. She kept walking as she pulled the phone out of her purse. It was her sister, Stephanie, and she sounded upset. "I've been trying to reach you, Nick. Why didn't you tell me?"

"Tell you what?"

"That you got your inheritance."

"No, I didn't," Nicole said. "The government took it all. You know that."

"That tabloid, *XHN*, is running an item about it. They say Blair's house finally sold, and you got $2.2 million." Steph gave a brief laugh. "Funny thing. They ran a photo of the two of us. The story's also on the *L.A. Times* website. No picture, though."

"That's crazy," Nicole said. "I haven't gotten a cent. Look, I'm on my way to the office. As soon as I get there, I'll look into it and let you know where they got the information." She groaned. "Imagine the begging letters I'm going to get. I'll make them publish a retraction."

Once in her office, Nicole went online to check her bank balance. To her astonishment, a deposit of $2,227,300.32 had been made into her checking account the previous Friday and had posted this morning. How had this money turned up in her checking account without her knowledge? Even the amount didn't make sense. Who had arrived at that figure and why had she gotten it?

True, she had been left a fortune the year before. Her benefactor, Robert Blair, had been the in-house investigator for the law firm where Nicole was office manager at the time. To Nicole, Blair was just a casual work buddy she occasionally lunched with. Only after his murder did she learn he'd been obsessed with her and had made her the beneficiary of an estate worth $5.2 million. But there was a catch: he'd made his fortune by blackmailing L.A.'s most powerful elite.

Nicole didn't want Blair's money. She regarded it as tainted, dirty. So she wasn't upset when the IRS had stepped in and put a hold on the estate until Blair's four million dollar house sold and taxes were collected on his illegal, unreported earnings. Soon after, the state of California informed her that anything left after taxes would go to the state's Victim's Restitution Fund, which is what often happens with criminal proceeds. When she learned this, she'd felt relieved, as if a great burden had been lifted.

She looked on the website of the tabloid *XHN*, which stood for "extra hot news." The story Stephanie had mentioned was easy to find, second from the top under a photo of Nicole and Steph. The item was little more than a caption, just a few lines about the inheritance. What upset her most was that both she and Steph were identified by name. It would have been bad enough if Nicole alone had been featured. But she felt much worse about the invasion of Steph's privacy.

She decided to call her attorney, Sue Price. Sue would be able to find out what was going on. She was just reaching for the phone, when it rang. The caller ID said it was Olympia Bank, which was on the ground floor of her office building and the holder of both her checking account and her new mortgage. She had no doubt what the call was about.

"Hey, Nicole. It's Kevin James down at the bank," he began. "We noticed something odd about your checking account, and the manager asked me to alert you. It might be a mistake but—"

Nicole knew Kevin from the times she'd gone into the bank to secure her mortgage. Although he was only in his early twenties, Kevin dressed in a suit and tie and had his own desk, putting him a notch or two above the tellers. He was tall and gangly with a soft voice and mild, affable personality. For reasons Nicole couldn't explain, he reminded her of a friendly giraffe—perhaps it was his height and hesitant manner. He seemed to take a special interest in her, always stepping over to chat when she came in or they ran into each other in the building's lobby.

"Thanks for the heads up," she said. "I already saw the deposit, and I'm looking into it."

"Okay," he said. "Uh, listen. The manager wants me to let you know that—well—if you've come into this much money, you should put it in some kind of investment fund so it will start producing earnings. The bank has a team of private wealth managers. Should I have one call you? It's only—"

"Thanks again, Kevin," she interrupted. "I'll think about it. Sorry, but I'm in kind of a rush. Bye, now." She hung up before he could continue. She hoped she hadn't been rude, but the last thing on her mind was finding a money manager. She needed to know why her checking account had been inflated with this huge deposit.

When Sue heard the news, she gave a whoop of delight. "That's terrific! You remember, don't you, that I contested the state's attempt to grab the whole estate? We'd already submitted a forensic accountant's report that showed Blair used his tax-paid wages to invest from the time he began working. He lived frugally, so he was able to accumulate two million perfectly legally."

Consulting the note where she'd written down the amount, Nicole corrected her: "$2,227,300.32."

"Right. I remember the thirty-two cents. Congratulations! That money is yours."

"But the state rejected your petition," Nicole said.

"They did at first," Sue said. "But I appealed, and it appears to have gone through."

"I don't understand. How was the money deposited in my checking account without my knowledge?"

"You signed a form with your banking information, remember? It was back when we first contested the government's attempt to grab the estate. It authorized a wire transfer of any amount due you into your checking account if our appeal was successful. Direct deposit is quicker. It also eliminates the danger of a check getting lost in the mail.

"What great news!" Sue went on. "This calls for some bubbly. Meet me after work and we'll celebrate."

Nicole hesitated. Being on the receiving end of Blair's money felt like anything but cause for celebration. "Thanks for being so diligent on this, Sue," she said. "I'd love to meet you, but I already have plans."

"Then let's set something up for another night," Sue said. "Wait, I have a better idea. We can meet for a celebratory breakfast at the Polo Lounge. That would give your good fortune the proper 'whoopee.' Looking at my calendar, next Wednesday's good. Does that work for you?

Nicole wondered if she'd feel any better about Blair's money by then. In any case, she'd have to go along with Sue's plan to celebrate. Sue had gone to a lot of trouble to make sure Nicole got the money, even if she didn't want it.

"Sounds good," Nicole said. "I'll make reservations for seven thirty. My treat."

Sue readily agreed. "You bet, rich girl."

As soon as they were done, Nicole called her sister and gave her the news.

"Gee," Steph said. "You sure don't sound very happy about it."

"You know I never wanted his money. I don't care if he did earn it honestly."

"Forget that jerk. This no longer has anything to do with him. The money is yours and it's going to change your life. Let's meet for dinner. David has to work late, so I'm free."

"Thanks, but I've got work to finish up and, frankly, I don't think I'll be very good company. When I'm done here, I'm going home, climbing into bed, and burrowing under the covers. Maybe it's being back in the tabloids, the fact that they put you in, too."

"Don't be upset on my account," Steph said. "I adore notoriety, and I love it that you're now rich and famous. Sleep on it. You're bound to feel better in the morning. Later!"

Nicole paused to consider whether a night's sleep was going to make any difference. She was about to say "later"—their usual signoff—but Steph had already hung up.

§

Brad and Ashley's house was in the Sunset Hills neighborhood a couple of miles north of Sunset Boulevard, which realtors called "Beverly Hills adjacent." The house, modern in design, was square and boxy. It was of pale-gray stucco with a single dark beam running across the front, marking the division between the first floor and second. The windows appeared dark in the glare of the midday sun.

Nicole got out of her car and approached the house. The front door was the façade's only distinctive touch. Made of cherry wood and perhaps ten feet tall, it featured a polished brass doorknob set in a curved bar of brushed copper. The hills above Sunset Boulevard may not have been Beverly Hills, but the area was pretty swanky. A house of this size was probably worth eight to ten million dollars.

That morning Nicole had called Antonia Gomez, Brad and Ashley's housekeeper. Antonia had agreed to meet with Nicole at 1:00 p.m. at the house where the couple had been living.

"Mr. Rexton's father asked me to stay on until the house is sold," Antonia had explained on the phone. She sounded young and had the hint of an accent. "Someone has to walk the dog, and he said it was better if the house was occupied. You know, to discourage burglars. It's good for me, since I was living here before—" She paused a beat before adding, "what happened."

The idea of staying alone in a house where a man was murdered and a woman kidnapped gave Nicole pause. She kept the thought to herself and agreed to drop by.

The doorbell triggered a loud onslaught of barking. A young woman opened the door, holding the collar of a large, white poodle. Antonia was tall, slender, and appeared to be in her mid-twenties. She wore her shiny, dark hair in a ponytail and had a welcoming smile. "Don't worry about the dog. She's very friendly. Sit, Champ." The dog obediently sat, still wiggling and wagging her tail. "Come in, come in," Antonia said. "Let Champ smell your hand and give her a pat; then she'll calm down."

Nicole did as she was told. Antonia released the dog, which came over to sniff the hem of Nicole's skirt. At Antonia's command, the dog sat again.

"Champ's very well trained," Nicole said.

"She should be. She's only a year old, but they had the trainer every week from the start so she wouldn't jump on Ashley and mess up her clothes. The dog's real name is Champagne, by the way. Silly, huh?"

Antonia led Nicole and Champ inside through a sky-lit entry hall. The living room, dining area, and kitchen were combined into a single room with a high ceiling. A wall of windows in back looked out over a swimming pool and, beyond that, the city. The walls and furnishings were in pale neutrals: whites, beiges and grays, accented by dark-brown furniture. A marble-topped table that could seat twenty occupied the dining area.

Nicole noted the abstract paintings Robert Rexton had mentioned. As she walked farther into the room, she caught sight of a huge bloodstain on the white carpet near the fireplace. This had to be where Brad had died.

Following Nicole's gaze, Antonia said, "No way that stain's coming out. Mr. Rexton is having a new carpet installed before they put the house on the market. Have a seat." She gestured toward an off-white sofa, one of three clustered in front of the big view window. "Would you like some coffee? Water?"

"No, thanks. I'd like to get started. First off, were you here when the break-in occurred?"

Antonia shook her head. "It happened on my day off, so I was at my mom's. The arrangement was for me to live here five days a week while I was working. That gave me Sunday and Monday off."

"And you found the body."

Antonia nodded, her eyes filling with tears. "It was a terrible shock. All that blood. And poor Brad. He was such a good guy."

"Where was the dog?"

"They locked her in the laundry room at night. They didn't quite trust her with the rugs. I'm sure she was barking her head off, but the neighbors are a ways off, and nobody heard anything. The break-in happened Saturday night, so the poor dog was locked up almost two full days. She left quite a mess in there."

"How long have you worked here?" Nicole said

"Almost a year," Antonia said. "Brad and Ashley were the best employers I ever had. I feel awful about what happened. Ashley was in charge of the house, and she was great. The last place I worked, the woman hovered over me, telling me what to do and how to do it. But I shouldn't badmouth her—Mrs. Reina. She was kidnapped, too, about a month before Ashley, and nobody knows what happened to her. Such a crazy coincidence! They were friends, and the same thing happened—" Antonia looked away and was quiet for a long moment before going on. "I mean Mrs. Reina and Ashley used to be friends. That was before Ashley hired me away from her. Then Ashley and Mrs. Reina had an awful fight, and they haven't spoken since."

"Did you tell the police that Ashley and Victoria Reina had been friends and that you used to work for Victoria?" Nicole said.

Antonia took a moment to consider this, then shook her head. "They asked so many questions it made me dizzy. But nobody asked about Mrs. Reina, and I didn't think of it. When Ashley offered me this job, I didn't hesitate. Mrs. Reina was a difficult person, and Ashley was so nice. She didn't care how I worked, or even how long, as long as the house was clean and the food was good. She was very appreciative." Antonia held out her arm to display a dainty gold watch. "She gave me this."

"Where's your room? Is it near theirs?"

"No. It's in back, on the other side of the house. I have a separate entrance."

"How were things between the Rextons? Were they close? Did they argue much?"

"At first, they were so lovey-dovey it could be embarrassing if I accidentally walked in on them. I'm talking about in this part of the house. I never went into their bedroom except when I was sure it was empty. But as time went on, things cooled off. Ashley was out a lot, shopping, lunching with her friends, and stuff. In the last couple of months, they weren't communicating much. I thought something might be wrong. But I never heard them argue. Not once."

"How much time did Brad spend at the house?"

"He was here most every day."

"He didn't go in to work?"

"Not much. Maybe once every few weeks. But his friends would drop by, and they'd swim and drink beer. Most days he'd lie by the pool or sit in that big chair and read." She gestured to a large mahogany-colored leather chair with an ottoman. "He'd usually fall asleep after a couple of pages. Since I've been working here, he never did finish the book he was reading at the start. It was about Muhammad Ali."

"Did they have many visitors?"

"They had a few dinner parties when I started. After that, they seemed to lose interest in entertaining."

"What about Ashley? Did she have people over?"

"Her decorator, Magda Stillman, was a regular. Ashley wanted to redo the kitchen, and they were working on that. They'd sit at the table and look through home decorating magazines."

"Did her relatives visit?"

"No. I think her parents were dead. She never talked about family."

"Any other visitors?"

"Oh, yeah, how could I forget? Her trainer, Chip, came every morning, Monday through Friday, at ten o'clock on the dot. Sometimes her women friends came in the afternoon and sat by the pool. I'd bring them drinks, usually white wine. Once in a while, Ashley would ask me to make a pitcher of margaritas or sangria. They liked that."

"What did they talk about?"

Antonia shrugged. "Boring stuff—clothes, diets, makeup, exercise, and household help—they were always hiring each other's gardeners, handymen, and pool cleaners. More than anything, they complained about their husbands. Once in a while one would lower her voice and talk about a man she was seeing on the side. I'm good at eavesdropping. But with these women, it wasn't worth the effort."

"Did Ashley complain about Brad or talk about other men?"

"Not when I was around. The women did tease her about how hot her personal trainer was. She just laughed and told them how great he was. Some of them did hire him."

"About the trainer—where did he and Ashley work out?"

"They used the pool house."

"Can you show me?"

Antonia got up, fetched keys from a drawer in the kitchen, and led the way. She unlatched the sliding glass doors. They stepped into the afternoon heat and walked to the edge of the redwood deck where a flight of stairs led down to the pool. They turned left and headed for the pool house. It was actually a wing of the main house with a separate entrance. Antonia unlocked the door and Nicole followed her into a sizeable room. Weights were lined up along one wall, along with a stair-stepper machine and an elliptical trainer. A small kitchen was equipped with a microwave, cappuccino maker, and mini-refrigerator. A bathroom and shower were visible through an open door at the back. Against another wall was a neatly made bed.

The bed caught Nicole's eye, and she noticed Antonia looking at it, too. "I'm going to put this as tactfully as I can," Nicole said. "Did you have to make up this bed very often?"

Antonia hesitated, as if reluctant to answer. Finally, she said, "Often enough."

"I understand you want to protect Ashley's reputation, but would you mind telling me how often?"

Antonia met Nicole's eyes. "Once or twice a week."

"How long did these training sessions last?"

"Two hours, sometimes more. Ashley really did work at keeping fit."

"Did Brad mind when she was in here with Chip?"

"Not that I could see. I don't think he was the jealous type.

Actually, he seemed to like Chip. Called him 'buddy' and would offer him a beer as he was leaving. Chip would always refuse, explaining that he didn't drink."

"What's Chip like?" Nicole said.

"I didn't like him," Antonia said. "He couldn't walk past me without patting my butt or groping me. I tried to keep my distance. And there was something shifty about him. He was always talking about how he and a couple of friends were planning an exclusive gym and spa. They were looking for investors. I think he was angling to get money from Brad or maybe Ashley. I told the police about him. I said, 'If I were you, I'd take a good look at Ashley's trainer.'"

Nicole got up and handed Antonia her card. "If you think of anything else, give me a call."

On the way back to work, Nicole considered what Antonia had told her about the women sharing—sometimes stealing—each other's household help, yard maintenance workers, and Chip, the personal trainer. Any of these people might be considered suspects. Even Antonia, nice as she seemed, could have enlisted others to help out with a get-rich-quick scheme like kidnapping wealthy women. Nicole wondered if the police were aware of this. She herself couldn't tell them; as a private investigator, her research and interviews were confidential, available only to the person who hired the firm to investigate, in this case Robert Rexton.

§

As soon as Nicole got back to her office, she thumbed through Ashley's phone book until she found Chip. He was under "L" for Chip Levin. She put in a call, but only got his voicemail, and left a message.

She went back to the beginning of the book and flipped through, noticing quite a few entries with area codes in other parts of the country. No one was listed under A except for

Antonia. The first name under B was a Dirk Baker, whom she reached on her first try. She explained who she was and that Ashley's father-in-law had hired her to find Ashley's next-of-kin.

"I wouldn't know anything about that." His voice was hushed and sounded as if he was trying to avoid being overheard. "I read about what happened in the paper. It has nothing to do with me. I hadn't seen her in months, and it was just a couple of times."

"Look, I'm not with the police," Nicole said. "Mr. Rexton's father just wants to find out if she had family somewhere. How did you know her?"

There was a click, and he was gone. From that brief conversation, Nicole was pretty sure she knew what kind of relationship Dirk Baker had with Ashley. That, and the apparent trysts with the trainer, made it look as if Ashley got around. She made more calls from the list, getting a third of the way through the book without reaching a single person. A number of calls had gone to voicemail while others rang until she hung up. A good half-dozen were no longer in service.

She was between calls when her phone rang. It was Chip.

After she explained what she wanted, he said. "Yeah. I heard, and I'm completely bummed. They were great to work for—the best. Ashley herself was a kind and generous woman, and she had a great bod. I'm a training professional, and she deserved a lot of credit because she really worked at it, dude, and it showed."

Being called "dude" as well the remark about Ashley's "bod" made Nicole pause before going on. "I understand you spent a lot of time with Ashley. Would you be willing to meet and answer some questions about her?"

"Sure," he said. "Anything to help. I'm pretty busy during the day, but how about we meet after work? I'm free tonight. Maybe we could have dinner, you know, on your employer's dime."

"I have plans for the evening," she said. "But we could meet for a drink. My office is in mid-Wilshire near the County Museum. Where are you?"

"I'm in Sunset Hills right now. Just name a place. I can be there by, say, six o'clock."

"How about the Blue Cellar on La Brea. It's about a half mile east of the museum. You need the address?"

"I know the place. See you at six-o'clock. Psyched about meeting you."

Remembering what Antonia had told her about Chip, Nicole didn't share his enthusiasm, but she knew how to handle men like him.

She got to the Blue Cellar a few minutes early to make sure she wouldn't have to share a booth with Chip. Instead, she commandeered seats at the bar and sat down to wait.

She knew who he was the moment he walked in. Tall, blond, and deeply tanned, he was dressed in a tight white t-shirt that showed off his impressive muscles. He was wearing tan chinos and boat shoes with no socks.

"I've just ordered white wine," she said. "What would you like?"

"Just water, thanks. But make it bottled, okay? None of that swill from the tap."

"What can you tell me about Ashley's past?" Nicole said. "Did she ever talk about where she came from, who her parents were, if she had any siblings?"

"We didn't get personal like that. It was just about what exercises she should be doing and how many reps. I did coach her on nutrition, like avoiding alcohol, but I got the feeling she wasn't interested."

"Did she ever talk about her friends, people she knew?"

"Uh-uh. See, I was just her physical trainer. I worked for her—you know, like the gardener. She wouldn't talk to me about stuff like that."

"What about her husband? Did she ever talk about him?"

"Not much. That Brad—hell of a nice guy. I still can't believe what happened. Do you know if they've found Ashley?"

"I don't think so." Nicole asked a few more questions but got the same "I-wouldn't-know-about-that" response from Chip. She studied his face. He had to be lying. He saw Ashley just about every day, spent several hours with her, and the two of them were probably having sex. He had to know more.

He rested his elbow on the bar and shifted toward her. "Let's talk about Nicole Graves," he said. "I've been reading about you and that money you inherited. If you're looking for a good investment tip—"

"Look," she said, cutting him off. "I'm here to find out if Ashley had any family. Isn't there anything you can tell me?"

He shrugged. "Why don't we get out of here? Maybe I'll remember something later."

She put down her glass and picked up the check, which the bartender had left on the counter. "Unless there's something you can tell me about Ashley, we're done."

But he was no longer listening. The bar was starting to fill up. Several attractive, well dressed women had just settled into a nearby booth, and he was watching them. They were in their late thirties or early forties, at least fifteen years Chip's senior.

He glanced at her and gave another shrug. "Whatever. I thought maybe you called because you wanted to hook up."

Nicole didn't bother to hide her irritation. "I found your number in Ashley's phone book." She stopped talking when Chip got up and walked past her toward the women in the booth.

Nicole paid the bartender and left.

On the way home, she remembered the fortune sitting in her checking account. She didn't understand why the money upset her so much, but it did. A feeling of dread settled in her stomach whenever she thought about it. But want it or not, the money was hers. Eventually, she'd have to deal with it.

She dragged herself through the evening, feeling exhausted but too stressed out to imagine she'd sleep if she went to bed early. She tried to read, but her mind kept shifting back to the previous year and the way she'd come into Blair's unwanted bequest. At other moments, she wondered how *XHN* had learned of her recent windfall—down to the exact amount—before she found out about it.

At last she went to bed and tossed fitfully, sleeping on and off until her eyes popped open and she was wide awake. The clock said 3:10 a.m., and she was sure she'd heard a noise. She hopped out of bed and went into the living room. Sure enough, someone was in the hall just outside her door, doing something to the door that made a rattling sound. She could also heard the low sound of voices. That meant there was more than one person out there, and they were trying to break in.

Nicole reached into her purse on the entry hall table and pulled out her gun. The ad for her condo had billed it as in a "security building," but she'd noticed there were two hefty deadbolts on the front door, as well as a sturdy chain lock, which suggested that whoever lived here before hadn't considered the building that secure.

"I've called the police," she called through the door, "And I've got a gun."

That was all it took. There was a moment of silence before she heard the men running toward the elevator. Nicole got her phone from her purse and dialed 911.

A squad car arrived within minutes, sirens blaring. Nicole buzzed them into the building. By the time they arrived at her door, several of her neighbors were in the hall wanting to know what had happened. Nicole explained about the would-be intruders, and one of the police officers told the residents to go back in their units and lock their doors.

The cops—there were two of them—were clean-cut, polite look-alikes, young enough to be fresh graduates of the police academy. After listening to Nicole's story and establishing that the men hadn't managed to break into her place, one of them told her they were going to search the premises. "Stay inside," he said, "and keep your door locked until we get back."

About fifteen minutes elapsed before they were back. The one who seemed to be their spokesman said, "We looked everywhere, and there's no sign of them. Does the building have CCTV?"

"Not at the moment. The building is switching security services. New equipment is supposed to be installed this week. So far it hasn't happened."

"Too bad," he said. "We'll file a report. There's not much else we can do."

"Thanks for coming out," Nicole said.

"Thank *you* for reporting it," he said. "We've had a number of recent break-ins in the area. Our records show there was one in this building several months ago. We think a single pair or gang may be responsible. Your report could help us establish a pattern leading to their capture. You've got good, strong locks on your door. Be sure to use them when you're home and when you leave. They'd make it pretty hard for a burglar to get in."

After they left, Nicole looked at the clock. It was almost five o'clock a.m., and she was wide awake. She made herself a pot of coffee. This was one morning, she thought, she'd be able to treat herself to a leisurely breakfast and have time to read the paper.

# THREE

WHEN NICOLE ARRIVED AT THE OFFICE, the receptionist said, "You have a visitor." She pointed to a man who got up from where he'd been sitting and stepped forward. He was tall with slightly tousled, dark hair. He might have been handsome if he hadn't looked so exhausted. He needed a haircut and was badly in need of a shave.

"Detective Greg Arnault," he said, reaching out to shake her hand. "And you're Nicole Graves. Read about you in the tabloids last year. I'd know you anywhere."

"My moment of fame," she said, looking up at him. "Glad that's over." She was fairly certain he was here because of the Ashley Rexton case, but she decided to play dumb.

"I need just a few minutes of your time," he said.

"Certainly. How can I help you?"

"Is there somewhere we can talk privately?"

"Of course. Follow me."

She led him into her office and gestured toward a chair facing her desk. "Have a seat." Then she noticed he was looking at the papers on her desk—case files that were strictly confidential. She quickly gathered them up and stacked them on a filing cabinet behind her.

"Something there I might be interested in?" he said. "Not to worry. I can't read upside down." His tone was jocular, and he smiled. Then his expression grew serious and he added, "The old man hired you, didn't he? Robert Rexton is convinced his daughter-in-law faked her own kidnapping, and his son died trying to save her."

"Do you think that's what happened?" Nicole said.

"You know I can't discuss an ongoing investigation. But I will say that we've looked into the MO of the perps, and it fits the pattern of the earlier kidnappings. Judging by the state of the bedroom, she put up one hell of a fight before they took her."

"Except this time someone got killed, and the victim hasn't been found," Nicole said.

He nodded. "True, but the second victim is also still missing. Other than that—"

"Why do you think there's been no further calls for ransom?"

"If the perps killed Brad Rexton, they'd be afraid to call and make demands. Our best theory is that they forced Mrs. Rexton to empty her bank account at various ATMs. Maybe she got a look at them while they were driving her around. If she could identify them, it makes sense they'd want to get rid of her."

"You think she's dead?"

He shrugged noncommittally. "If that's what happened."

"Aren't there cameras outside banks? Wouldn't you able to verify if Ashley herself was at those ATMs?"

"I've already said too much. I can assure you we're investigating every lead. But I'm the one who's supposed to be asking questions."

"Go ahead," she said.

His expression darkened. "I have to ask you to stand down. Stop poking your nose into our case. It's possible you might alert a suspect and undermine our investigation."

"Do you have a suspect?" she said.

He ignored the question. "These are very dangerous people. I'm here to warn you. Don't mess with them."

"All I'm doing is looking into Ashley's background. I'm not interested in finding the kidnappers or even Ashley herself. Her father-in-law, Robert Rexton, was her only known next of kin. He hired me to track down her family, if she has one, so he can let them know what's happened. On our databases—and yours, too, I'm sure—her records go back only six years. Are you looking into that?"

"Again—I can't comment," he said, somewhat irritably, "but let me be clear. For your own safety, stay away from this case. And see if you can convince your firm to drop the investigation." When he got up, she stood, too.

They made eye contact, and for a long moment, Nicole found herself unable to look away. His expression had softened, and she felt a connection that had nothing to do with what they'd been discussing or the request he'd just made. At last, the spell broke, and he turned to leave.

Before reaching the door, he turned back, pulled a card from his pocket, and handed it to her. "If you do stumble across any information," he said, "I'd appreciate a call."

"Sure thing," she said.

He opened his mouth as if to say something else, then changed his mind and left, closing the door behind him.

Nicole stood there, considering his mixed message: Stay away from this case, but, if you find out something, let me know. He had no legal grounds for making her stop looking into Ashley's past. And he knew, just as well as she did, that she was going to keep looking until she found out more about Ashley or ran out of places to look.

Once Detective Arnault was gone, Nicole set about calling more people in Ashley's phone book. She was able to reach a dozen women who'd met Ashley through a husband or boyfriend who was close to Brad. Each said more or less the same thing: that she didn't know Ashley well and had no idea of her family connections, the kind of work she might have done, or anything else. Some had been part of Ashley's lunch crowd or included in her shopping sprees. Several mentioned that Ashley rarely talked about much except celebrities, fashion, cosmetics, and fitness.

Nicole gathered that what Rexton senior said about his son was true: Brad was well liked. He was considered "fun to hang out with" and "a great host." Several mentioned his lack of ambition but excused this as the result of growing up as a trust fund kid. "Why should he have to work if he didn't feel like it?" one woman said. "He was rich."

The last woman Nicole reached summed up what the others had said about Ashley: "She was kind of an enigma. Beautiful? Yes. Everyone could see Brad was nuts about her, but she never revealed anything about herself. She was pleasant enough, but there was something deeply impersonal about her."

"Like she was hiding something?" Nicole asked.

"I didn't think that," the woman said. "But she always kept herself at a distance. I couldn't figure out where she was coming from, what she liked or didn't like, her plans for the future. You know, who she really was."

Nicole understood. She'd encountered women who'd been deeply unknowable in just that way. They stuck to superficial conversation and never revealed anything personal. It was as if they'd constructed a wall that made it impossible for anyone to get close.

Except for a short break for lunch, she worked nonstop for the rest of the day. By the end of the afternoon, she was almost done with Ashley's address book, but she still hadn't found any new information.

§

Nicole was deeply asleep when the ring of her phone went

through her like an electric shock. It rang a second time as she fumbled to find it on her night table. The illuminated face of her alarm clock said it was 3:20 a.m. When she turned on the lamp, she saw that the phone had fallen to the floor. She leaned over to pick it up and hit the answer button, but the other party had hung up. She figured it was probably a wrong number from someone in a different time zone but decided to check to be sure. She brought up the list of recent callers and was surprised to see her sister's name at the top of the list. Her call had come in less than a minute before. Nicole called back, but the phone went to voicemail. She concluded Steph was still on the phone, leaving a message. But why would she be calling so late? What could it possibly be that couldn't wait until morning? Over the next few minutes, Nicole checked and rechecked her phone messages. Nothing.

She called Steph again and then a third time, but no one answered. When she tried Steph's landline, the answering machine picked up. Nicole was wide awake by now and thoroughly alarmed. Why would her sister call at this hour and then not answer either phone? Steph had abandoned her cramped, run-down apartment for her fiancé's comfortable, roomy one several months ago. David, Steph's fiancé, would be there, too. Why hadn't he picked up the phone if Steph was in the bathroom or something? Nicole looked up David's cell number and called him. He didn't pick up either.

Almost without thinking, she was up, pulling clothes from her closet. She'd go over there and make sure everything was all right. Then she remembered that Steph kept her phone under her pillow with the ringtone turned off, using a headset to listen to soothing music while she fell asleep. She'd probably rolled over and accidentally pushed a button on the phone. It could have triggered a call to Nicole—the pillow equivalent of a butt call.

That would explain why Steph hadn't answered her cell, but why hadn't anyone answered the landline? Maybe, she told herself, Steph and David, wanting uninterrupted privacy, had unplugged the house phone and turned off the ringtones on their phones. Somewhat reassured, Nicole climbed back into bed. But her heart wouldn't stop thumping, and she couldn't shake the feeling that something was wrong.

These fears tumbled about in her head until the sky began to grow light. She'd just dropped off to sleep when her alarm rang. It was six o'clock. Normally, she rose at seven o'clock. But she'd promised to meet Sue for their celebratory breakfast. Before getting up, Nicole tried calling Steph again. Still no answer, but that was understandable. Her sister never rose before nine o'clock. If she'd turned off her phones the night before, she'd still be unreachable. In the light of morning, Nicole's nighttime panic seemed a little silly. She'd get in touch with Steph later, and they'd figure out what had happened.

Wearily, Nicole got out of bed. Once again she felt as if she hadn't slept at all. A long hot shower and a cup of coffee somewhat revived her. When she was ready, she drove up to Sunset Boulevard, entered the grounds of the huge, sprawling pink complex that made up the Beverly Hills Hotel, and left her car with the valet. Even though she'd lived in L.A. her whole life, this was her first visit to the famous Polo Lounge. Despite its reputation as a celebrity hangout, she'd always considered it more of a tourist trap than a dining destination. But, as she walked in, she had to admit the place was beautiful. The lavish planters, green walls, and green and white striped ceiling gave the place the feeling of a well-tended garden. It also smelled incredibly good with the sweet, cinnamon aroma of something baking.

At seven thirty a.m., the place was almost full, but, as Nicole looked around, she didn't spot a single celebrity. Sue was already there and had managed to snag a large corner booth. They greeted each other with a hug, then consulted the menu and ordered an elaborate breakfast to share: eggs Benedict with butter-poached Maine lobster, a wild mushroom omelet, and the Polo Lounge's special bakery basket. The lobster Benedict was forty-seven dollars, the omelet thirty-two dollars, the pastry basket twenty-four dollars—crazy prices for breakfast. But this was the Polo Lounge. And, after all, Nicole thought, the fact that she was getting part of her inheritance was due to Sue's legal maneuvers, for which she refused to accept payment.

They ordered and were waiting for their food when Nicole's phone rang. She pulled it out of her purse.

"Nicole—Oh my God!" The voice was so hoarse she didn't recognize it at first. "I've got to talk to you. Where are you?" It took a long moment before she realized it was David, her sister's fiancé.

"I'm in Beverly Hills having—"

"Go home. I'll see you there in twenty minutes."

"Wait!" Nicole remembered the phone call during the night and felt herself go cold. "What's wrong? Is it Steph? Has something happened to Steph?"

There was no answer, just a dial tone. He'd already hung up.

"What is it?" Sue said. "You've gone completely white."

"I don't know." Nicole was finding it hard to breathe. She took in a gulp of air before she went on. "That was Steph's fiancé. He sounded hysterical. He told me to go home so he can meet me there. Then he hung up." She bit her lip, trying to keep from falling apart. "I think something has happened to Steph. I got a call from her in the middle of the night. I missed it and called back, but nobody answered. I thought it was strange."

"Don't jump to conclusions," Sue said. "You have no idea what this is about. Maybe she broke up with him or something. Do you want me to come with you?"

"No," Nicole said. "I've got it." As she stood up, the waitress arrived with a big tray of food. Nicole asked Sue to settle the check. "I'll pay you back," she added.

"Don't worry about it." Sue got up, grabbed a muffin and a Danish from the pastry basket, wrapped them in one of the

stood in the hall waiting. When David emerged from the elevator, Nicole was shocked by his appearance. The area surrounding his left eye was red, puffy, and swollen. Blood, dripping from his nose, was spattered down the front of his shirt.

When he reached her, he blurted it out, words tumbling over each other: "Some guys broke into our place last night and took Steph. I tried to fight them off, but there were three of them. They punched me, then hit me on the head."

Nicole went cold. For a brief moment, she felt as if she was going to faint. This passed as she experienced a wave of disbelief. This couldn't be happening. She held her breath, waiting for David to mitigate this terrible news with words like "but she's okay," or "she was able to get away from them."

But David was silent, looking desperately into her eyes. He seemed to be hoping for her to reassure him. All at once, the blood that had been trickling from his nose came gushing out, like water from a spigot. He put his sleeve against his face to stop the flow.

Nicole knew a little about nosebleeds, since her mother had been afflicted with them. "Sit down and tilt your head back as far as it will go," she said. "Then pinch your nostrils together."

David obliged, but when he tried to pinch his nose, he let out a yelp. "I can't put pressure on it. It really hurts."

"Maybe it's broken," Nicole said. "I'll get a towel and some ice. Then I'm calling the police and an ambulance. You need a doctor."

"No! You can't do that!" His bleeding nose made it sound as if he had a bad cold.

"We've got to call the police, David. The sooner they start looking for Steph, the more likely they are to find her before anything really bad happens."

"No police. These guys said they'd kill her if we called them." With that, he broke down, leaning forward with his head in his hands. Blood dripped from his nose onto his pants and the rug.

Nicole hurried into the kitchen and—hands shaking—

dampened a couple of dish towels, grabbed an icepack from the freezer, and hurried back to David.

"Lean your head back and put the ice on your nose while I clean you up." As she wiped his face and neck, she noticed blood on the couch behind him. She went around to get a look. Sure enough, there was a wound on the back of his head. Blood was dripping onto the back of his collar and from there onto the couch. By now the nosebleed had let up. She had him press the towel against the wound on his head while she went back to the kitchen for another icepack and more dishtowels.

She sat down next to him so she could take over applying pressure to his head. "Tell me exactly what happened."

"A little past three o'clock last night. I heard a noise." He stopped and gulped back a sob. Nicole thought of the call she'd received at 3:20. The hair rose on the back of her neck. Had Steph been calling her for help?

"We'd had a fight, so I was sleeping on the couch," David went on. "Steph was asleep. You know how she is. They could nuke the city, and she'd sleep through it. As soon as I opened my eyes I saw them. It was dark, but I made out three guys dressed in black hoodies and ski masks. They didn't say anything, just started toward me. I tried to fight them off, but it was three against one. I managed to punch one in the face. He hit me back. Meanwhile, one of the others came from behind and bashed me over the head with something. I think it was the poker from the fireplace. I must have passed out because the next thing I knew, I was on the floor, and they were tying me up.

"None of them spoke the whole time. Once I was tied up, they turned me on my side facing away from them and played a recorded message. I couldn't see where it was coming from; I'm guessing a cell phone. They repeated the same message three times to be sure I got it. It was a guy talking in falsetto to disguise his voice. The first thing he said was, 'Don't call the police or Stephanie will die.' The recording told me to give you a message:

You're to get twenty thousand dollars in bills no bigger than twenties and deliver them to a drop point in Centennial Park at eleven o'clock tonight, when the place is deserted. Centennial is a small rec area near the entrance to Griffith Park. There's a big fir tree with a hollow in the trunk. You're to put the money in there." He was talking fast, his words tumbling out. "The recording said they'll send you instructions for delivering the rest of the money—two million dollars—after they get the twenty thousand dollars. They knew your name and all about your inheritance." He paused to draw in a deep breath before going on. "After the last replay, one of them jabbed a needle in my arm, and I blacked out. Whatever it was kept me under for a few hours. It was almost light when I woke up. It took a long time to work my hands free. That's when I called you."

Nicole was quiet, taking this in and studying David's face. His injured eye had now turned purple and was swollen shut. The pupil in his right eye was dilated, almost filling his iris.

"Listen to me," she said. "I don't care what the recording said. We're calling the police. This has happened to three other couples. In two cases, the husbands paid the ransom without calling the police, and one of those wives is still missing. The LAPD knows how to handle this, and we don't. Besides, you need medical attention, so I'm also calling an ambulance. Your eye looks weird. You may have a concussion."

He went on talking as if he hadn't heard. "I've thought this over. There are private crisis management firms that take care of this kind of thing. The police want to catch the perp as much as they want to rescue the victim. These companies just care about getting the victim back. They negotiate with the kidnappers and give them what they want."

"We're not doing that," she insisted. "The police can bring in the FBI. They have all kinds of sophisticated resources. The LAPD itself has a great record at rescuing kidnap victims." She picked up the phone and punched in the numbers.

"Wait!" David said. "What if your phone is bugged?'"

"This is my landline. No way it's bugged. I never use it, and it's unlisted. I just have it in case of a blackout or an earthquake."

"What is your emergency?" a man was saying at the other end of the line.

"I want to report a home invasion and kidnapping, but I have to speak to a police officer before you send anyone out. The kidnappers said they'd kill my sister if we call the police."

"Hold on," he said.

Almost immediately another man's voice came on. "Who am I talking to?" he said. "Name and address."

Nicole gave him the information, then told him her sister had been kidnapped, but quickly added, "You can't send a patrol car. They've threatened to kill her if —"

"Got it. Tell me what happened and who was kidnapped."

Nicole did, repeating the basic facts David had told her.

"We'll be right out. We'll be discreet—unmarked car, no sirens." He repeated the address she'd given, "4157 Elm, Number 2B. That's an apartment, right?"

"It's a condo."

"Is the garage open?"

"No, it's a security building. Call when you get here. I'll buzz you into the garage. Take the elevator to the second floor."

"Is this where the kidnapping occurred?"

"No, my sister was taken from her apartment in Hollywood."

"And you know about it—how?"

"Her fiancé was there when it happened. He drove here to tell me."

"We'll need that address so we can send a team to investigate."

"You can't do that. The kidnappers might be watching."

"Yes, yes," His tone was impatient. "I'm aware of that. The team will be disguised as cable technicians or telephone repairmen; they'll arrive in an officially marked vehicle. Any chance there's a key hidden outside the apartment?"

"Steph keeps one on the molding over the front door—but the kidnappers may have taken it."

"No problem. There's always a way to get in. We're sending two detectives to your place. They should be there in a few minutes."

Once they'd hung up, she noticed David had dozed off. She reached over and shook him. "With that head injury, you have to stay awake. Now that the police are on their way, I'm calling an ambulance."

"No! I'm fine," he said. "What those guys gave me made me sleepy, that's all. I'm not going anywhere until I hear what the police are going to do."

"Okay, but you've got to stay awake." He nodded in agreement, even as his eyes started closing. She reached out and gave his shoulder another shake.

"Listen," she said. "You said you and Steph had a fight, and you were sleeping on the couch. What were you fighting about?"

He shrugged. "Everything. I don't know what's going on with her." His voice cracked. "Nicole, I think she may have gone off the idea of marrying me."

"That's impossible, David," Nicole said. "I talk to Steph all the time, and she hasn't said anything like that to me. She seems excited about the wedding."

"Yeah, I thought so, too, until a couple days ago. She told me we had to talk. So we sat down, and the first thing she says is that she doesn't think she's ready to settle down." He paused so long, it seemed as if he might be dropping off again. "No. That's not it," he finally said. "What she said was she wasn't ready to settle, which is a whole different thing, and it really shook me. Just a few days before, she acted like she couldn't wait to become Mrs. David Stevenson.

As Nicole listened, it sounded familiar. All her life, Steph had been in and out of relationships. Until David came along, she'd always refused to commit to much of anything, except the right to change her mind. Poor David, she thought. He's about to have his heart broken.

Nicole's focus immediately switched back to the danger her sister was in. Would the police be able to rescue her? Would they allow ransom to be paid for Steph's release? She'd read about the families of people kidnapped abroad and how the United States sometimes refused to allow families to pay ransom because it might encourage more kidnappings. Did the LAPD have a similar policy? The idea made Nicole even more anxious. She'd be happy to give up the money to save Steph.

David had gone silent, apparently absorbed in his own thoughts. Nicole went into the kitchen to get more ice and swap out the dish towels, now soaked with blood and melted ice. When she came back to swap out the towels and ice, she noticed the knuckles on his right hand were bleeding, too.

The phone rang. When she answered, a man said, "We're at the garage entrance." She could tell from his voice that this wasn't the same person she'd spoken to minutes before. She got up and pressed the button that opened the garage door. "We're in," he said. "See you in a minute."

Moments later, the buzzer rang, and she opened the door. Two plainclothesmen were standing there. She was surprised, then not surprised, that one of them was the detective who'd visited her office to warn her off the Rexton case.

"Detective Greg Arnault," he said, "Remember me? And this is another member of the team investigating the recent kidnappings, Detective Steve Jones." He gestured to the second officer who was only now coming through the door.

Arnault still looked exhausted. Aside from that, he was even more disheveled. His dark hair was uncombed, his shirt rumpled, and he now had designer stubble. He also gave off a negative vibe that hadn't been there before. Maybe it was just fatigue. It occurred to her that he and his team might be working around the clock, under a lot of pressure to solve these cases.

Detective Jones, whom she assumed was Arnault's partner,

was short, muscular, and compact. He had fair, buzz-cut hair and a sour affect. Nicole could picture him as a bully in his youth. As soon as he entered, he started wandering around, checking out framed photos on her mantel and the paintings on the walls before wandering down the hall toward the bedrooms. She was tempted to ask where he was going and why. But she held her tongue. All that mattered was Steph, getting her back.

Arnault glanced over at David. "And this is?"

David started to get up, winced, and dropped back onto the couch. "I'm David Stevenson, Stephanie's fiancé. I was with her when these men broke in and took her." His voice was shaky, and he looked as if he were about to cry.

"David," the detective went over to shake David's hand. Arnault's eyes widened slightly when he took in the bloody nose, bruised, swollen eye, and grazed knuckles. "Looks like you put up a quite a fight. You need medical attention?"

"No," David said. "I'm all right."

"Is it okay if we sit over there?" The detective pointed at the dining area where four cane-backed chairs were gathered around a large, round table. "It will be easier to record our conversation."

David managed to get up and make his way to the table, but he was clearly in pain. Arnault placed a small recorder on the table and turned to David. "Why don't you tell us what happened."

Nicole's stomach was churning. She couldn't bear this delay. She wanted the police out there now, looking for Steph. Of course, they had to hear what had happened first, but Arnault didn't seem to be in any hurry.

David told much the same story he'd told Nicole. The detective seemed especially interested when David said that he and Steph had a falling out, and he'd been banished to the couch.

Arnault asked several questions about the fight. "What were you arguing about?" "Do you and your fiancé often fight?" "Did you think she was about to break up with you?"

David gave a weary shrug to each question without answering.

Finally he said, "No, we hardly ever fight. This blowup last night? I don't—" he gave another shrug. "Something was bugging her—no idea what. But we don't fight. No, hardly—"

David's speech had become slightly slurred, and he seemed to lose track of what he was saying. Nicole could see his condition was deteriorating.

"You say these men were wearing ski masks and hoodies," Arnault said, "but can you tell us anything else about their appearance? Height? Weight?"

"Man, it was dark. I'd turned on the light in the hall. The switch for the living room is by the front door, so I couldn't — I just saw silhouettes."

"How did they get in?"

"Dunno. The front door was open. Maybe they picked the lock. I kept meaning to put in deadbolts but—"

"What happened next?"

"I told them to get out or I'd call the police. They walked toward me. I hit one of them, and he punched me in the face." David pointed at his nose and swollen eye. "Next I know," he went on, "I'm on the floor and they're tying me up. They didn't talk, not a word."

He described the recording the men had played for him, the request for ransom, the warning not to call the police, and the injection that had left him incapacitated until morning.

"How'd you get untied?' the detective asked.

"Worked the knot with my teeth. Then pulled 'til my hands—free. Took a long time."

"Do you mind holding out your arms? I'd like to see your wrists," Arnault said. The request set Nicole on edge. For the first time, she realized that David, as Steph's significant other, would be the police's first suspect.

David, resting his chin on his hand, didn't respond. His good eye was at half-mast as if he was about to fall asleep.

"Your wrists, sir," Arnault said in a louder voice. "Can I see them?"

As David reached his hands forward, the sleeves of his shirt hiked up to reveal a chafed ring of red around each wrist. Arnault got up and walked behind David's chair to take a look at the back of his head. "You're still bleeding," Arnault said. "You sure you don't want a doctor?"

David sat up, suddenly alert. "What I want is for you to get to work looking for my fiancé."

"That's what we're doing, sir. First we have to hear how she was taken. Any details you can give us about those men will help."

"That's all I remember. As soon as I got myself untied, I called Nicole," David said. "I was afraid to call the police because they said not to. But Nicole, here—she convinced me it was the right thing."

"Why'd you drive all the way over here to tell her? You could have done it by phone."

"I don't know," David shook his head and was quiet a beat, as if considering it. "Guess I wasn't thinking straight."

The detective turned to Nicole. "What about the ransom they're asking—two million and change. You got that kind of money?"

Nicole nodded. "Funny thing. That amount was wired into my account a few days ago. It was my inheritance from Robert Blair. You know about his murder case. You mentioned it when you visited my office. Two days ago, the tabloid website *XHN* ran a story saying I'd received money from the estate. Anyone could have seen it."

"So, you have the means to pay the ransom?"

She nodded.

"Did *XHN* specify the exact amount?'

"Yes. I have no idea how they found that out. But they have tipsters all over, and they're not above hacking into phones and computers."

"Okay," Arnault said. "Here's what's going to happen. You go about your day as usual, except you'll go to the bank and take out two thousand dollars in twenties."

"They said twenty thousand dollars," Nicole said.

"No way we're putting twenty thousand dollars out there. We have a protocol for this. We'll supplement the real twenties with blanks to make it look like the right amount. Otherwise, you'll follow their instructions and make the drop tonight. Law enforcement will be hidden near the drop point to protect you. They'll be careful not to be seen. Once these clowns pick up the money, our men will follow them to where they're holding your sister. Don't worry. We'll get her back. They're not as smart as they think they are."

As Arnault stood up, his phone rang. He made a few grunts in response to what was said on the other end. Then he hung up and looked at David. "Our forensic guys are going over your apartment now. They say there's no sign of forced entry." He turned to Nicole. "They found your sister's phone. It was under the bed. The last number she called, at 3:20 a.m., was yours. Did you speak to her at that time?"

"No," Nicole said. "By the time I got to the phone, she'd hung up. I called her back on that line, their landline, and David's cell, but no one answered. It worried me, and I almost went over there, but—" She stopped talking. Why hadn't she followed her first instinct? It might have made a difference. By the time she got there, of course, the kidnappers would have already taken Steph. Still, the police could have started looking for her right away instead of hours later.

"We have a few more questions," Arnault told David. "We'd appreciate it if you'd come down to the station so we can continue our conversation."

"What are you talking about?" Nicole said. "This man needs a doctor."

Arnault turned to her, his face expressionless. "He says he's fine, and he's declined treatment twice. If we keep him talking, he may remember more details that will help us."

"Well, he's not fine." Nicole said. "His nose is probably broken, and he may have a concussion." David was silent, the lid of his good eye starting to droop, as if he was drifting off again.

"Will you excuse us for a minute?" Nicole said. "I want a word with him."

Arnault and his partner stared at her, as if they hadn't understood.

She went to the front door and opened it. "Please," she said, "step out into the hall so David and I can speak privately." Arnault seemed puzzled by this request. But after some hesitation, he and his partner walked out into the hall. Nicole closed the door after them.

"Listen to me," she told David. "Whether you think so or not, you need medical attention. You've told the detectives everything you remember, right?"

He nodded. "But some of it's still foggy. Like, I think Steph called something out, but maybe I dreamed it. If I keep talking, I might remember—"

"It's not a good idea to keep talking to the cops. When I let them back in, you're going to tell them you want a lawyer."

David looked at Nicole in confusion. "Why would I want a lawyer? I just want to help them find Steph."

"As her fiancé, you're their first suspect."

"That's ridiculous!"

"Of course it is, but that's how cops think. You've told them what you remember. Now you need legal advice. We'll call my lawyer. She's really good. When I let them in," she said, "say you've asked me to call an attorney and refuse to answer any more questions. If you remember something that might help with the case, your lawyer can relay it on to them. Other than asking for a lawyer, don't say another word."

As she talked, David's eyes closed.

She gave him a shake. "Did you hear what I said about the

lawyer?"

"Yeah," he muttered, beginning to drift off again.

Nicole shook him again. "You've got to stay awake." She let the detectives back in, and David drowsily told Arnault that he wanted a lawyer. By now, his speech was so slurred that he sounded drunk.

The detective gave Nicole an accusing look, one eyebrow raised, then turned to David. "Is this what she told you to say? Don't you want to help us find your fiancé? Believe me, we're all on the same page here. We're hoping you can remember more details to further our investigation. You're not a suspect."

"Lawyer," David mumbled.

Arnault turned to Nicole. "Look, Ms. Graves," he said. "I know you want your sister back, but this isn't helping. She may end up suffering because we weren't able to complete our interview of Mr. Stevenson. His memory is foggy. We could—"

"You heard him," Nicole said, pulling her cell out of her purse. "I'm going in the other room to call his attorney. I'll also be calling 911. He's obviously in need of a doctor."

Detective Jones, who'd been standing by listening, suddenly turned, walked into the hall, and disappeared into the bathroom. Nicole imagined him going through the contents of her medicine cabinet.

Meanwhile, Arnault reached into his pocket, pulled out his phone, and handed it to her. "Don't use your cell," he said. "It might be bugged. Use mine instead."

Nicole took the phone into the kitchen, but she kept the door open so she could make sure Arnault didn't keep prodding David with questions. She called 911 and asked the operator to send an ambulance. Next, she called Sue. Although Nicole tried to keep it brief, it took a while for her to explain. Sue agreed that David needed protection from further questioning. She promised to send someone to sit with him as soon as Nicole let her know where the ambulance was taking him.

When Nicole got back from making her calls, David was fast asleep with his head on the table. Once again, she woke him up. Arnault had settled on the couch. She gave him back his phone. He took it but made no move to get up. Clearly, he wasn't planning to leave anytime soon.

# FOUR

STEPHANIE SLOWLY RESURFACED from a deep sleep and opened her eyes. Her mind was in a fog; she had no idea where she was or how she'd gotten here. Dim light leaked in through three small windows located high on the wall, but they did little to illuminate her surroundings. All she knew was that she wasn't in her own bed, and she was freezing.

She wondered briefly if she might be dreaming, but the cold and the dank, moldy smell of the place were frighteningly real. Panic clutched at her, the need to get away. She sat up and felt around for something to cover herself so she'd stop shivering. But all she had was a single blanket, no sheets. The buttons of a cheap mattress dug into her.

The last thing she remembered was waking up to the sounds of a scuffle and a loud thud from the direction of the living room. David's side of the bed was empty. She'd started to get up—and then what? Nothing.

A wave of drowsiness almost overwhelmed her, but she

resisted. Forcing herself to swing her legs over the side of the bed, she wrapped the blanket around her shoulders and stood up. The sudden movement made her so dizzy she immediately sat back down. She tried again, this time easing herself up more slowly. Still off balance, she stumbled forward until she reached a wall. She leaned against it, using it for support as she moved forward in search of a light switch. Only when she stubbed her toe did she realize her feet were bare. No wonder she was so cold; the floor felt like cement, and it was freezing. She became more cautious, taking smaller steps to propel herself along. The wall was cold, too, with a rough texture. Her best guess was that she was in a basement. But what basement? Their apartment house just had underground parking. Questions ate at her, fueling her sense of panic. Where was she? How had she gotten here? All of her instincts told her that she had to flee before something terrible happened.

Just then she bumped into the bottom step of a staircase hidden in the shadows along the wall. A wave of nausea hit, and she felt as if she was going to pass out. She braced herself against the wall to keep from falling and stood there until the worst of it passed. The basement had grown a little lighter. Looking up, she could make out a door at the top of a steep flight of stairs. That door must be the way out of here. She put her foot on the bottom step and reached for the railing. As soon as she touched it, a spiderweb grabbed onto her hand and clung to it. She did her best to wipe it off on her nightgown. The dizziness returned, and she realized she was too wobbly, too depleted to make it up the stairs.

She reversed direction and worked her way back to the bed. It took everything in her to keep going. This effort made her panic recede. Several times, she thought she was going to faint. At last her shins bumped into the side of the bed. With a sense of relief, she lay down, pulled the blanket from around her shoulders, and used it to cover herself. The thin layer did nothing to warm her frozen feet. Despite her fear and discomfort, she instantly fell asleep.

# FIVE

THE PARAMEDICS ARRIVED WITHIN a few minutes of Nicole's call. She'd been trying to keep David awake while they waited, but it was a losing battle. Along with that, his nose was bleeding steadily.

After taking his vitals, the paramedics packed his nose with gauze, a process that made Nicole wince, although it drew no response from David. She wondered if he was still conscious. Once they were done, they put away their equipment, unfolded a compact bundle into a stretcher, and lifted him on.

Arnault was busy on his cell. Jones had emerged from the bathroom and was crouched in front of Nicole's bookcase, scanning titles. Occasionally he'd pull out a book and flip through some pages. She wondered if this was his role—snooping around the homes of people being questioned—or if he was new, unsure of his duties, and too green to be trusted with actual work. Arnault didn't seem to be paying attention to what Jones was doing. Maybe he didn't care.

Once David was loaded onto the stretcher and belted in,

Nicole said, "Can I ride along with him?"

"Sorry," one of the paramedics said. He was unusually tall, like a basketball player, with a narrow face and Brillo-curly brown hair. He seemed to be in charge. "We only allow that for parents of injured children. We'll be taking him to Cedars, which is the closest emergency. You can drive over there and leave your car in emergency parking."

She felt a hand on her shoulder and turned to see Arnault. "It would be best if you didn't go to the hospital," he said. His tone was more conciliatory, his expression sympathetic. "You need to go about your business as if nothing happened, remember? Once Mr. Stevenson is on his way, I want to ask a few questions. Then I'll explain what's going to happen next. Okay?"

Nicole nodded. Past experience had made her wary when a cop said he "wanted to ask a few questions."

The paramedics started to carry David out, and the tall one turned to her. "I don't think he's in any danger. But he might have a concussion, so it's good you called us."

David's eyes were still closed. "Is he unconscious?" Nicole said.

"I'm not sure, but I think he's asleep. Do you know if he's taken any drugs? He seems to be under the influence of a fairly powerful sedative."

"The people who assaulted him gave him an injection of some kind to knock him out. I have no idea what it was," she said.

"His vitals are good. They'll check out the head injury when he gets to the hospital. Don't worry. They'll take good care of him."

As Nicole followed the paramedics into the hall, she noticed her neighbor Dorothy standing there, watching the drama play out. Dorothy lived on gossip about her neighbors. Several times she'd cornered Nicole to dish the dirt about people who lived in the building, people Nicole didn't even know. Nicole wondered how long she'd been there and how much she'd overheard. Once the paramedics disappeared into the elevator, Nicole gave Dorothy a wave, went back in her condo, and closed the door.

restaurant's dark-green cloth napkins, and handed the small bundle to Nicole. "Let me know what happened."

Nicole rushed out to the valet. As soon as her car arrived, she placed the napkin-wrapped pastries on the seat next to her and headed for her condo. It took seven minutes, speeding down from Sunset and heading west along Wilshire. She was gripping the steering wheel so hard her fingers started to cramp. She tried to relax and calm down. Maybe Sue was right. It might be nothing more serious than a lovers' quarrel. But, if that was the case, why would David turn to her?

Steph's decision to accept David Stevenson's proposal had come as a pleasant surprise. Through high school, college, and ever since, she'd gone through an endless series of slacker boyfriends—some so objectionable they made Nicole worry about her sister's safety. Twice Steph had been forced to get restraining orders after breakups. As she did with all of her sister's suitors, Nicole had checked David's background through the Internet and her firm's database. He had a degree in computer engineering and a well-paid job with one of the country's biggest Internet companies. Good credit, no arrests, a model citizen.

As for appearance, David was tall, six-foot-three to Steph's five-eleven, and they made a striking couple. He wasn't handsome in the conventional sense, but he had nice blue eyes and a square jaw that made him look as if he'd stepped out of a Marine recruiting poster. What impressed Nicole most was his benevolently take-charge attitude. It was clear that he was going to look out for Steph and keep her safe. Most important, he clearly adored her, quirks and all. In the months David and Steph had been together, Nicole had grown fond of him.

Once Nicole got to her place, she spent the next fifteen minutes pacing, waiting for David to arrive. At last the phone to the building's intercom rang. She pressed the button, and David's voice came through, sounding breathless. "It's me."

She buzzed him into the building, opened the front door, and

"Where do you want to sit?" Arnault said. "At the table?"

Nicole gestured toward the couch. "Why don't you sit there?" She chose the upholstered easy chair she used for reading. It was a little higher than the couch and brought her up to Detective Jones's eye level and almost up to Arnault's. She felt the added height gave her a strategic advantage.

"I feel we got off on the wrong foot," Arnault was saying. "I apologize if I was a little aggressive." Jones nodded his head at her, either agreeing that Arnault had been aggressive or offering his own apology. He still seemed distracted, eyes scanning the condo.

"No worries," Nicole said. "But I know what you're thinking. David is your first suspect. You wanted to keep him talking as long as you could, hoping he'd say something incriminating."

"I can see why you might think that," Arnault gave her a disarming smile. "But you're mistaken. Mr. Stevenson isn't a person of interest. We don't have enough information to draw any conclusions, but I understand. You've had experience with this kind of thing. As I said before, our first concern is finding Stephanie. So, we're all on the same page. Right?"

Arnault had dropped the negativity he'd walked in with and was now playing good cop or, perhaps, the role of sympathetic friend. Even though she still didn't trust him, she was picking up some kind of the chemistry between them. At a time like this, it was not only confusing but disturbing. She looked away, not wanting any part of it.

"Before we go any farther," she said, "I want to point something out. David's interest in Stephanie has nothing to do with money. He's been with Steph for about nine months. I have a job, but— at least until a few days ago—I was just managing. Steph herself is a freelancer, and she struggles to make ends meet. As for my inheritance, that came as a complete surprise. I was told I'd get nothing. David was never after our money. I want to make that clear."

"Appreciate the information," Arnault said, "But how well do you really know Stevenson? He may not be the nice guy you think he is."

"Just for the sake of argument," she said, "suppose he was involved. Why would they beat him up like that?"

"You never know," he said. "It might have been staged, and they went after him a little too hard. Let me ask you this: Don't you think it's odd that you were looking into the last kidnap victim, and the same thing happens to your sister?"

"It is odd. Any thoughts?"

"Maybe it's a copycat crime set up by someone who knows you."

"I think I explained that an article about my inheritance appeared in *XHN* a few days ago. It disclosed the amount," Nicole said. "Anyone could have seen it."

He seemed to discount this possibility. "Think about it, okay?" he said. "Is there anybody you know whose behavior raises questions?"

Nicole thought of what had happened the night before, the attempted break-in. Had the kidnappers been after her? Failing that, had they decided to take Stephanie?

When she told Arnault about it, he asked. "You got CCTV in this building?" Once again, she explained that the building was temporarily without it.

"I'll look up the police report on the attempted burglary," he said. "It may have just been a coincidence. Anything else?"

Nicole remembered what Antonia, the Rexton's housekeeper, had said about Chip, and the fact that Ashley's friends relied on each other's recommendations for household help. She couldn't tell Arnault that Antonia had previously worked for Victoria Reina, the other missing victim. That would violate the confidentiality rule of her trade. Any information gathered during an investigation could only be released to the person who'd authorized it. After a beat of hesitation, she came up with a compromise. "What about the Rexton's household help? I understand that Ashley and her friends often used the same housekeepers, personal trainers, pool cleaning services, gardeners, and handymen."

"Believe me," Arnault said, "we're taking a look at everyone who came into contact with the Rextons and the other kidnap victims. If there's overlap, we'll find it. One more thing: I'd like the names of people you interviewed while looking into Ashley Knowles' background."

"You already have them. Rexton gave the police copies of Ashley's address book and daily diary, which I used for my contact list."

"I haven't seen them," he said. "But I'll track them down. Do you mind if I ask some questions about your sister?" At Nicole's nod, he went on. "Are you two close?"

"Yes. Very."

"How often do you talk?"

"Usually every day, sometimes more than once. Plus we often get together on weekends."

"When did you last talk to her?"

"Last night, around eight o'clock."

"What did you talk about?"

"She told me about a hotel she and David had looked at for their wedding. She seemed fine. But we didn't talk long. She was carrying on a conversation with David at the same time she was talking to me. I figured they wanted time together."

"So he was in a hurry to get her off the phone?"

Nicole felt a surge of annoyance. He was twisting her words. "I didn't say that. They're in love. If it had been me, I'd rather be making conversation or whatever with my fiancé than talking to my sister. That's why I kept it short."

"Did she mention seeing or hearing from any of her old boyfriends?"

"Old boyfriends?" This gave Nicole pause. "No."

"I checked her on our database. She has two restraining orders against men who were harassing her."

"That was a while back," she said. "One was at least five years ago. Until she met David, she used poor judgment in choosing boyfriends. But she hasn't heard from either of those guys since the restraining orders. At first, they couldn't believe she was breaking up with them. But once she made an official complaint, they accepted it. Do you think one of them might be responsible?"

"We're not ruling anything out. Did she mention any threats, strangers hanging around her building or following her? Anything unusual at all?"

Nicole thought about it. "Nothing. She'd been caught up in wedding plans and rarely talked about anything else. I was surprised to hear that she and David had a fight last night. I think that may have been a first. But let me ask you a question."

"Sure."

"These recent kidnappings," Nicole said. "Do you think Steph was taken by the same people?"

"At this point, I have no idea. Once our techs finish going over your sister's place, we'll know more. By the way, these cases are very unusual for us. The LAPD rarely gets reports of adult kidnappings. Most involve children, and the vast majority are really custody beefs between parents.

"About the Rexton case, the one you were looking into, here's what I can tell you."

Arnault repeated the same information she'd read in the paper. In fact, she'd gotten more from the conversations she'd had with Robert Rexton and Antonia.

When he was done, Nicole said, "Has there been any news about the other missing kidnap victim—Victoria Reina?"

Arnault sighed. "All I can say is we're putting all our resources into investigating these cases and locating the missing victims."

"That means you can't comment, right? Even if you were onto something, you wouldn't tell me."

"Here's what we're going to do," Arnault said, evading the question. "Jones and I are going back to the station to see if we can dig up any leads. You go about your day as usual except that at some point you'll visit your bank and take out the money. Try not to worry. These guys are amateurs. We'll get her back."

He pulled a card from an inside pocket. The strap of a gun holster was visible when he opened his coat. He jotted something on the card and handed it to her.

"You already gave me your card," she said.

"This one has my cell number on the back. Don't hesitate to call if you remember anything or need my help. One more thing. On your way to work, stop at a convenience store and get a burner phone. Call me with the number. Don't use that phone except to communicate with me. This afternoon we'll send someone to your office to package the money and prepare it for the drop. What time do you leave work?"

"Since I've missed most of the morning, I'll stay at least until six o'clock."

"Expect a plainclothes detective to drop by sometime this afternoon."

Nicole went to the door to see the detectives out. Once they were gone, she gathered up her purse and jacket and looked around for anything she might have forgotten.

Waiting for the elevator, she glanced out the hallway window, which allowed a view of the street. David's car was parked in a no-parking zone, and a ticket was waving from his windshield wiper. Instead of going down to her car, she stopped on the first floor and went outside.

She reached under the passenger-side fender. She and Steph had used David's car to go shopping the previous month when Steph's car was in the shop. Steph had left the keys in the ignition and locked them out of the car. She'd called David, almost in tears. David had patiently explained that it wasn't a problem because he'd hidden a key for such a mishap. It was taped inside a fender.

Nicole had been meaning to do the same with her own car but hadn't gotten around to it.

She drove David's car into the garage and parked it in her spare parking space. She put the key back where she'd found it and got into her own car.

She felt shaky and sick with worry about Steph, at a loss as to how she could get through the day pretending that nothing was wrong. Had she done the right thing calling the police? What if the kidnappers found out? What would they do to Steph? Nicole couldn't shake the feeling she'd made a terrible mistake.

# SIX

STEPHANIE WOKE WITH A START. Sunshine was leaking through the small, high-placed windows that were her only source of light. Her watch said ten thirty. It was still morning.

She pulled herself out of bed and, a little steadier on her feet, made her way to a closed door she hadn't seen earlier. She opened it and flipped on the light. A single bare bulb emitted just enough light so she could see spider webs in the corners. Careful not to touch them, she used the toilet. There was no soap, hot water, or towel. She rinsed her hands, splashed some cold water on her face, and wiped her hands on her nightgown. The water and cold cement floor made her shiver so much her teeth began to chatter.

She pulled the blanket from the bed and, using it for a wrap, headed for the stairs leading up to the closed door. The staircase was rickety, and quite a few steps were so weak that they buckled slightly when she put her weight on them. She went up slowly, one step at a time, gripping the handrail. At the top, she saw that an uneven, square slot had been cut in the door. It was covered by what looked like a crudely made flap on the other side. Beneath the opening, a piece of wood, held up by brackets, formed a slightly crooked shelf.

She tried the door. Finding it locked, she started beating on it, screaming, "Help!" and "Let me out of here." There was no response. She stopped pounding when she noticed a light switch on the wall next to the door. She flipped it, but nothing happened. Looking around, she spotted a single light bulb, dusty and burned out, suspended from the ceiling on a long cord. She turned her attention to the flap that covered the opening in the door, pushing on it. Nothing happened. It seemed to be locked from the other side.

She resumed pounding on the door. "Hey!" she yelled. "I'm cold and hungry." She banged and shouted until her voice was hoarse, but the place was silent. At one point, the floorboards overhead creaked, raising her hopes. When the sound stopped, she decided it was probably just the house settling as the day warmed up. Exhausted by her efforts and sick with fear, she started back downstairs. She was halfway down when a noise behind her made her look up. The slot in the door opened, and something slid onto the shelf from the other side.

She hurried back up to find a tray holding a mug, a bowl with a spoon in it, and a folded sheet of paper. The tray was brown plastic and looked as if it had been stolen from a cafeteria. She started to pick it up, then reconsidered. With the tray in her hands, she wouldn't be able to see where to put her feet as she descended the stairs. A fall onto the cement could be the end of her. Instead, she tucked the note under her arm, picked up the cup, and climbed down.

She sat on the bottom step and took a sip from the cup. It was coffee, floating with loose grounds. Someone had made it camp-style, boiling coffee grounds in a saucepan. Although it was bitter, it was nice and hot. She sipped it greedily, holding the cup with both hands to warm them. She drank it all before setting the mug down. Only then did she pull out the note to read it. She had to hold it up to catch the light. The message was written in block letters on lined paper that appeared to have been torn from a notebook. It said, "You can stop yelling. Nobody can hear you. Just stay put and don't try to escape. All we want is the money. Don't make us hurt you."

The mention of money puzzled her only for a moment. She didn't have more than a couple of hundred dollars in her account, but Nicole did. A lot of it. These people had kidnapped her to get at Nicole's bequest. At first, the idea was hard to process. She'd read about three recent kidnappings. One victim had been released, but the other two had not. Were the same people who'd taken her responsible for the other kidnappings? She had no doubt Nicole would part with the money to buy her freedom. At the same time, she wondered if her captors would let her go once the money was paid.

Her nose was running from the cold, and her immediate discomfort took over her thoughts. She was freezing, and she wanted more coffee, a hot meal, some blankets, and a coat or jacket to wear over her thin nightgown. She had to figure out a way to communicate with her captors, who seemed determined not to interact with her. If she had a pen, she could write her requests on the back of this note and slip it under the door. But no such luck.

Now, in the dim light that reached her, she saw that the basement didn't have four solid walls. On one side was a crude partition of wood slats. She went over to peer between them. What she saw was the dark crawl space under the house. This was the source of the moldy smell. Some distance away, an open vent of some kind admitted a small amount of light. It occurred to her that she could crawl over to the vent and see if it was big enough to squeeze through. But the smell told her it was damp under there. She couldn't imagine herself worming her way through damp soil that might be riddled with spider webs and rats' nests.

Instead, she braved the stairs again and resumed banging on

the door. "It's freezing down here. I need more blankets, hot food, something warm to wear, and another mug of coffee," she yelled. Then, even louder, "Please!"

There was no answer. As she was standing there, she heard a door slam and the sound of a car start up and drive away. Were they leaving her alone here? She beat on the door again, screaming, "Don't leave me like this!" But the house was silent.

With a sense of defeat, she took the bowl from the shelf and carried it back downstairs. The bowl contained some kind of cold, sugar-coated cereal—frosted flakes, as it turned out—soggily floating in milk. Despite the cereal's lack of appeal, she ate every bit of it. When she finished, she felt a little better. She sat awhile, trying to calm herself so she could figure out what to do. If she were Nicole, she thought, she'd already have picked the lock and escaped.

All at once, she felt irresistibly sleepy and all thought of escape evaporated. She lay down on the bed, wrapped herself in the blanket, and—still cold—went back to sleep.

66

# SEVEN

As soon as Nicole pulled out of her garage, she pushed the button on her steering wheel to activate her phone and called her office. Joanne, Nicole's closest friend at work, answered.

"My car won't start," Nicole lied, "I'm waiting for the auto club. They're really busy right now, so I might not make it in for a while."

"I'll spread the word you'll be in late," Joanne said. Her voice was muffled, as if she had her mouth full. "Anything urgent on your desk?"

"Nothing," Nicole said. "Whatever it is you're eating sounds good." She could picture Joanne, plump and always talking about whatever new diet she was on, making the morning's exception with a cookie, leftover birthday cake, or some other treat from the break room.

There was a pause while Joanne made chewing noises. "No. It's horrible. Some gluten-free protein bar Jerry's been raving about. He brought in a box and left it in the break room like a carton of doughnuts. But it's, like, the worst." There was a pause before she continued. "There, I spit it out. When you get here, steer clear of Jerry's High Octane Bars. See you!"

Her call to the office out of the way, Nicole set out on her errands. She stopped at a tiny convenience store for a burner phone and, once back in the car, used it to call Arnault. He didn't pick up, so she left a message with her new phone number.

Her next stop was the bank on the first floor of her office building. She filled out a withdrawal slip for two thousand dollars and got in line to wait for a teller. That was when she noticed Kevin James motioning her over to his desk.

When she shook her head and pointed to the row of tellers, he got up and came over. "You don't need to wait, Nicole," he said. "I'll be happy to help you."

Just then, Nicole felt a hand on her shoulder. It was the bank's manager, James Blagg. She'd been on Blagg's radar ever since she first opened an account. He'd recognized her from the previous year's headlines and seemed to regard her as some kind of celebrity.

Reluctantly, she followed Blagg into his office. The special treatment he lavished on her took a lot more time than waiting for a teller. In Nicole's opinion, Blagg was a little off. He dressed in the traditional bank manager's uniform, a navy suit of undistinguished tailoring, a striped tie, and a light blue shirt. But the outfit clashed with the way he wore his dark hair sticking up in spikes, a do that could only be accomplished with a liberal application of styling gel and time spent primping before a mirror. Worse yet were his large, brown-leather, plug-style earrings, which fit in with the hair, but not the suit. She wondered how recently upper management had gotten a look at him.

"Have a seat, Nicole," he said. "How can I help you today?"

"I need to make a withdrawal," she said, handing him the withdrawal slip. "I'd like it all in twenty-dollar bills."

He studied the slip a moment and flashed her a smile. "Feeling generous today, eh?"

She looked at him in consternation.

"It was a jest," he said. "Now that you've come into some wealth, I was suggesting you might feel magnanimous enough to give a handout to some of our homeless." He tilted his head at her, smiling, waiting for her to get the joke.

Nicole failed to return his smile, and he blustered. "None of my business, of course. Wait here. I'll get the funds you requested."

When he was gone, Nicole looked around his office, wondering if anything new had been added since her last visit, when she signed the final papers for her mortgage. There were still no family photos or clues to any hobbies. Instead, a couple of generic landscape paintings graced the walls. His sole personal touch was a framed certificate that occupied a small easel on his desk. It said he was a member of Mensa, the society whose only requirement was an IQ score in the 98th percentile or higher. She had noticed Blagg never used a short word when a long one would do. She glanced at the certificate and wondered, once again, why anyone would need to broadcast this information to others.

As Nicole waited, she grew impatient. She was late for the office and itched with the impulse to get up and leave. But, no, she had to pick up this money. She sighed and sat back in her chair.

Finally, Blagg returned with a stack of bills. He counted them into piles and tapped each pile on the desktop to even up the edges before combining them into a single stack. Then he went about tapping the edges again. Finally, he fastened the stack with a rubber band and handed it to her.

"Thanks," Nicole said, getting up to leave.

Blagg gave her big smile. "Have a great day, Nicole. I mean it."

"Same to you, James," On her way out of the bank, she retrieved a deposit envelope from the supply station. Realizing that all of the bills wouldn't fit into a single envelope, she pulled out another. She divided the money in half, stuffed it in the envelopes, and shoved them into her purse. She was glad she'd thought to bring along her largest handbag. Aside from the envelopes of money, her wallet, and sunglasses, the bag contained a small cannister of pepper spray, her keys, cell phone, and the new burner phone. At the bottom was her gun, a small Smith and Wesson revolver. She couldn't decide which she hated most, the gun or target practice. Even so, she'd felt compelled to carry a weapon after a couple of brushes with violence. And practice was an absolute necessity. If she was to carry a gun, she had to know how to use it.

By the time Nicole arrived at the office it was twelve thirty, and the place was deserted; everyone had gone to lunch. She closed her office door, took the money out of her purse, and locked both in the full-length cupboard where she kept her coat and personal property.

She sat down and stared at her computer screen for a while, unable to focus on work. Her mind kept slipping back to Stephanie and what she might be going through. Nicole refused to consider the idea that Steph might already be dead. It was bad enough that her sister was a kidnap victim, who might be tied up in the trunk of a car or in an abandoned basement or a warehouse somewhere, terrified about what might happen next.

Would the kidnappers hurt her? Rape her? Kill her? Nicole's thoughts went back to the first time she held the newborn they were to call Stephanie. At the age of seven, Nicole had been thrilled at the thought of a little sister, even when people reminded her that she wouldn't be the baby anymore. She remembered Steph as a toddler who followed her around and called her "Nini." The grown-up Stephanie was now five-foot-eleven and towered over Nicole. Even so, Nicole had never gotten past the idea that it was her job to watch out for Steph and protect her. Now, look what had happened. Tears welled up in her eyes and spilled down her cheeks. Would she ever see her sister again?

Nicole went into the bathroom, dried her tears, and splashed cold water on her face. Once she returned to her desk, she forced herself to take another look at the little information she'd gathered so far.

Rexton said that Ashley claimed she was born in the Philippines, the daughter of a United States serviceman. Nicole went to the website where government records were stored. After a bit of searching, she found a registry of births to service members stationed abroad between 1950 and 2012.

Ashley's records said she was twenty-eight, and Robert Rexton had said that before marrying into the Rexton family, her name had been Ashley Rose Knowles.

Nicole skipped down to the Ks, and bingo, there she was: Ashley Rose Knowles born to Sgt. First Class Alphonse Knowles and Alicia Beckman Knowles, August 28, 1991. Manila, PHL."

The record carried a link. She clicked on it and found herself looking at an image of the actual birth certificate. She took a screen shot and printed it out. This proved nothing, of course, but Nicole felt she was getting somewhere. She now had the names of Ashley's parents. How many Alphonse Knowles could there be? He should be easy to track down. If he was still living, maybe he'd be willing to tell her something about Ashley. Even if he wouldn't answer questions, he and Ashley's mother deserved to hear what had happened to their daughter.

Before she had a chance to follow up, her phone rang. It was the guard downstairs asking permission to admit a Greg Arnault. Nicole gave the go-ahead. A few minutes later, Joanne, who'd just returned from lunch, showed up at her door with Arnault in tow.

"Greg here was looking for your office," From Joanne's smile and pink cheeks, it was clear she found the detective attractive.

In fact, Arnault had cleaned up surprisingly well. He'd recently shaved, and his hair was neatly combed. He was dressed in khakis and a checked shirt with the sleeves rolled up, like the techies who showed up when an office computer went haywire. What he didn't look like was a police detective.

"Hey!" His voice was flirtatious. Nicole had to admit that she liked this version of Arnault a lot better than the one she'd met before.

"Hey," she said, ushering him into her office. Joanne was still standing there, eyebrows raised. Nicole flushed as she closed the door on Joanne and her curiosity.

Arnault was carrying a black computer bag with a shoulder strap. He gave her a long, unreadable look before saying, "Let's get to work." Without asking permission, he scooped the papers on her desk into a single, disorderly pile, shoving it aside. She was annoyed, thinking about the time it would take to get the papers back in order.

Arnault set his bag down and pulled out stacks of newsprint cut in the same size as paper bills. "I'll need the money you withdrew to make bundles of twenties."

"Here, I'll get it for you." She unlocked her cupboard and pulled out the envelopes from the bank. She watched while he made stacks of the fake bills with a handful of real twenties at either end. Next, he bundled each stack with an official-looking magenta band marked $2,000.00. He did this deftly, like an experienced player shuffling a deck of cards. When he was done, he had ten bundles of bills. He put them into the computer bag he'd brought and handed it to her.

"This is ready for the drop," he said. "Since you have no other way to communicate with these people, I want you to put a note in the bag. Tell them you need proof of life before you hand over any more. Ask for a photo of your sister holding up the current day's newspaper."

He studied Nicole's face a moment, then added, "Don't let this add to your worries. It's just protocol. We have every reason to believe Stephanie is alive, and we'll bring her home safe. I also want to assure you we'll be looking out for you when you deliver the money. We'll follow you from the time you leave home—discreetly, of course. More officers will be staked out at the park." He put his hand on her shoulder. "I know how hard this is. How are you holding up?"

She felt tears welling up. "No sympathy, please, or I'll turn into a puddle."

"That's completely understandable. Go home and try not to worry too much. We'll wait for the kidnappers to show so we can follow them. If they don't go directly to where they're holding your sister, we'll wait until they do. When you go to bed, keep the burner phone nearby. But don't expect to hear from me until morning."

Shortly after he left, there was a knock on her office door. It was Joanne. "Who was that?"

"Just a computer tech. My machine's been acting up."

"Wow," Joanne said. "My computer's misbehaving, too. I sure wouldn't mind a visit from this guy. Unless you're interested."

"No, no," Nicole said. "Of course not."

"Great. I'll call Computer Solutions and ask for him."

Nicole thought a minute, fearing her lie was catching up with her. She toyed with the idea of telling Joanne what had happened to Steph and that Arnault was a detective working on the case. He'd warned her not to tell anyone, but she knew she could trust Joanne with a secret. On the other hand, Nicole didn't want to burden anyone else with her troubles.

She decided to improvise. "Actually, he doesn't work for Computer Solutions. They were booked for the day, so they had to farm out the job. I have no idea where he works."

"That's okay," Joanne said. "I'll call Computer Solutions and find out."

"I'll do it," Nicole said. "They always send a follow-up message asking for an evaluation of the tech's work. I'll let you know." She figured she'd wait and, if Joanne asked again, explain that Greg's employer was a competitor of Computer Solutions, and the company wouldn't tell her where he worked.

After Joanne was gone, Nicole returned to her desk and sorted through the papers Arnault had displaced, arranging them back in proper order.

This accomplished, she located her printout of Ashley's birth certificate and searched the office database for an Alphonse Knowles. Sure enough, there was only one person listed by that name. His last known address was in Long Beach, about forty minutes south of L.A. According to the record, he was still with Alicia, the woman listed as Ashley's mother. A phone number was given. Although these numbers were often out-of-date, it was worth a try.

The phone rang five times. She was about to hang up when a man said, "Hello." He sounded impatient, as if he was certain this was a nuisance call.

"Hello. I'm calling about Ashley —"

Before Nicole could say more, there was a click, and she was disconnected. She immediately redialed.

The same man answered. This time his voice was an angry growl. "What do you want?"

"I'm terribly sorry to bother you," she said. "But is this Alphonse Knowles?"

"What business is it of yours?"

Despite his hostile tone, she went on, "Are you the father of Ashley Knowles?"

"Who is this?" he fairly shouted.

"My name is Nicole Graves. I'm a private detective. I have news about Ashley—"

"Don't ever call this number again," the man said before slamming down the phone.

Wow, Nicole thought. Something bad must have gone down between father and daughter. This man wasn't going to tell her anything.

Leafing through her notes again, she ran across mention of Ashley's brief stint working for an orthopedic clinic in Albuquerque. Nicole looked up the clinic's website to find the phone number. The place was run by a Dr. Charles Carson.

A woman answered with, "Carson Orthopedic Clinic. How

may I assist you?"

"I'd like to speak to Dr. Carson," Nicole said.

"May I ask what this is in regard to?"

"It's personal."

"You'll have to give me more than that. Dr. Carson is a very busy man."

"It's in regard to Ashley Knowles."

Moments later, Dr. Carson was on the line. "I hope Ashley didn't have the nerve to use me as a job reference," he said. "If you're considering hiring her, I'd advise you very strongly against it."

Playing along, Nicole said, "May I ask why?"

"She isn't trustworthy," he said. "I'll just leave it at that."

"Surely you can tell me more. She didn't work for you long. Did she leave without giving notice?"

This triggered a reaction from Carson. He drew in a breath and said, "Worse than that. She disappeared with money she embezzled from my practice."

"Did you report her to the police?"

"No."

"Why not?"

Instead of answering, Carson hung up, a response that spoke volumes. Her best guess was that Ashley had something on him. Perhaps she'd manipulated him into a compromising situation before she made off with his money. If Carson didn't want whatever it was to come out, he wouldn't report her to the police. This reinforced the idea that Ashley was a grifter. Still, it revealed nothing about where the woman had come from or what she was doing before she went to work for Carson.

This had been Nicole's last lead. She was more than disappointed. She remembered Rexton's contention that Ashley had staged her own kidnapping. If that was true—and Nicole was becoming convinced it might be—Ashley must be out there somewhere, desperate for money to get away and assume a new identity. She wasn't getting the big payout she'd hoped from her husband's trust fund. If she resurfaced, pretending her kidnappers had let her go without a ransom, that would raise a lot of questions. Ashley couldn't afford to have the police take a close look at her background.

Nicole wondered if Ashley had been behind Steph's kidnapping. She thought back to the night when those men tried to break into her own place. Maybe Ashley had seen the article about the inheritance and sent her accomplices to kidnap Nicole to make her hand over the money. When that failed, had they focused on taking Stephanie instead? The idea made Nicole feel sick.

If she could find out more about Ashley, it might provide a clue to Stephanie's whereabouts. Even though the police were on the case, Nicole told herself she couldn't stop digging.

Alphonse Knowles had refused to talk to her. But people were often willing to open up to her in person. It was one of the times when her appearance was an advantage. What people saw was a petite, harmless-looking woman with a dimpled smile.

She decided to drive down to Long Beach and pay a call on Alphonse. Waiting for news about Steph was making her crazy. She had to be doing something—anything that might lead her to her sister, and finding Ashley might be the key. What if she was hiding out with her parents?

Nicole glanced at her watch. It was two forty-five. She could be in Long Beach by three thirty or so, depending on traffic. If she went now, she'd be home by dinnertime. Maybe Knowles would slam the door in her face, but past experience told her he might very well invite her in.

First, she printed out a photo of Ashley to bring with her, so Mr. and Mrs. Knowles could confirm that this was indeed their daughter. Nicole told Jerry where she was going, got directions to the Knowles' house, and set off. Traffic was light, although the bumper-to-bumper tie-up on the opposite side of the freeway told her the trip home would be a long one.

Alphonse and Alicia Knowles lived in a modest but well-kept house on a cul-de-sac in a small enclave of look-alike tract homes. They were all flat-roofed, 1960s modern. The street, devoid of parked cars, looked deserted. She parked in front of the Knowles' house and rang the doorbell. A white-haired woman, who appeared to be in her sixties, opened the door and quietly pointed to a sign over the mail slot that said "No Soliciting, Fundraising, Politics, Salesmen, Religion."

Nicole smiled. "I'm not here for any of those," she said. "I called, but couldn't reach anyone, so I drove down from L.A. Are you Mrs. Knowles?

The woman nodded. She appeared tentative, as if debating whether to shut the door or invite Nicole in.

"I believe you'll want to hear what I have to say. Can I come in? This won't take long."

"Who is it?" a man yelled from the back of the house. Nicole recognized Alphonse Knowles' voice. He sounded just as angry as he had on the phone.

Mrs. Knowles stepped out onto the porch and closed the door behind her. "He has a heart condition and a bad temper to boot. I don't want him all riled up. Just tell me what it is and be on your way."

"It's about your daughter, Ashley. She was kidnapped about a week ago, and she hasn't been found. The police are looking for her."

At the mention of Ashley, the woman looked down, and her face went slack, as if she were about to cry. She was silent a moment before she said, "We have no daughter. Years ago, we had a beautiful baby girl we named Ashley Rose. She was born with a heart defect and lived less than a week." The woman gave a sniff and wiped her eyes before looking up again. "We were never able to have another child. This woman, whoever she is, must have gotten a copy of Ashley's birth certificate and used it to steal her identity. We've gotten calls, people looking to find this 'Ashley,' whoever she is. All we can make of it is that she's some kind of con artist. The disrespect these people show when they call—it really upsets Al."

Nicole pulled the photo out of her purse and handed it to Mrs. Knowles. She stared at it a long moment, narrowing her eyes, then looked up at Nicole. "I think I know who this is. She was the daughter of our next-door neighbors at one point. Her name was Jessica, and she was still in her teens. I remember because she was about the same age Ashley would have been. She gave her parents no end of grief. I think she ended up in juvenile hall."

"Do you remember the family's last name?" Nicole said.

Mrs. Knowles bit her lip, looking into the distance. Finally, she said, "I'm sorry but I've forgotten. We moved around a lot before Al retired from the service."

"Would you have mentioned the death of your daughter to neighbors?"

"Probably. People are always asking how many children we have. It would be easier just to say we don't have any, because it's painful to talk about. But that would be like denying Ashley Rose ever existed. It feels wrong to me."

"I can understand that," Nicole said. "I'm so sorry to have brought this reminder to your door." She waited while Mrs. Knowles dabbed at her eyes again before going on. "You said this girl, Jessica, was a teenager at the time, the same age Ashley would have been. According to Ashley's birth records, she would have been twenty-eight this year. That means these people would have been your neighbors sometime between eleven to fifteen years ago. Does that sound right?"

Just then, the front door opened, and a man Nicole presumed was Alphonse Knowles was staring at her with open hostility, his face flushed.

"Al," Mrs. Knowles said. "This nice lady has figured out who stole our Ashley's identity. She drove all the way down from L.A.

to let us know. Show him the photo, Nicole."

Nicole handed it over to him. His anger faded as he studied the photo. "She does look familiar, but I can't remember where I've seen her."

"Her parents were our next-door neighbors some years ago," Mrs. Knowles said. "Her father was tall and thin. I believe he was a master sergeant, the same rank as you at the time. I'm pretty sure this girl's name was Jessica. Can you remember the family's last name?"

Alphonse drew in a breath and, after staring at the photo a bit more, said, "Yeah, I remember that guy. His name was Gleason or maybe Meese. Something with an 'ee' sound to it." He turned to Nicole. "Can you do something to make her quit using Ashley's name?"

"I doubt she'll keep doing that," Nicole said. "Not with the police looking for her." She explained again that the woman calling herself Ashley Knowles had been kidnapped and was still missing. "I think you've given me enough information to find her real identity," she went on. "Thanks so much for your help."

After they all shook hands, Nicole gave them her card and asked them to call if they remembered anything else. Soon she was back on the freeway. At home, she had the Knowles's address for each of their moves. It would take time, but she was pretty sure property records would yield up the name of the neighbors with a daughter called Jessica.

She listened to the news on the drive. After a bumper-to-bumper hour-and-a-quarter on the freeway, she made it back to her neighborhood at five thirty. She stopped at Whole Foods to put together a meal from the food bar. Normally, the first thing she did when she arrived home was to call Steph and see how her day had gone. Realizing there could be no such conversation brought tears to her eyes. Arnault seemed sure tonight's stakeout would lead them to Steph. But what if it didn't?

Nicole was in the checkout line when her phone beeped with

a new message. Getting out her phone, she saw there were in fact three messages, two of which had come in earlier. They were all from Sue's young associate, Melanie, who appeared to have spent the day at the hospital with David. In the first message, Melanie said David had been sent for an MRI of his head. The second, which had arrived around noon, said David was being taken into surgery to relieve pressure caused by swelling of his brain. The last message said he was out of recovery but still hadn't regained consciousness.

Nicole left her groceries in the cart, got her car from the lot, and headed for the hospital. Arnault had advised her to forego visiting the hospital. But David was almost a member of the family, and she felt guilty for not checking on him earlier. In her anguish over Steph, she hadn't given him a thought. He'd been able to drive to her place that morning, and the paramedic had been so reassuring. She'd never considered his injury might be serious.

She trolled the neighborhood around the hospital, hoping to find street parking. When nothing materialized, she entered one of the crowded parking structures surrounding the huge medical complex. She had to drive round and round until she reached the roof level before she found a space to leave her car.

The chilly, disinfectant-laden air of the hospital made Nicole even more anxious. She had to locate David and make sure he was all right. She blamed herself that he was here. If it hadn't been for her inheritance, this never would have happened. Robert Blair's generosity—if you could call it that—was the reason Stephanie was taken and David was injured. If only she could go back in time and not befriend a man who neither wanted nor needed friends.

She approached the information desk and was directed to another wing of the building. Following a maze of corridors, she had to ask for directions several times. It seemed as if she'd parked at the farthest possible point from David's room. The size of the place and its long, twisting passageways were disorienting. At last she found the right floor in the right wing of the building. She checked at one of the nurses' stations for directions to his room. A pert-looking nurse, whose name tag said Mindy Schwartz, checked something on her computer and said, "I'm afraid we're only admitting immediate family and—" She paused to look at her computer. "His lawyer."

"I'm David's sister-in-law," Nicole said, stretching the truth a bit. "My sister, his wife, was kidnapped." These words, spoken for the first time to a stranger, brought tears to Nicole's eyes. "So, I guess I'm the most immediate family member you're going to get.

Mindy reached out and put a hand on Nicole's shoulder. "I'm so sorry! You'll find him in room 708, bed A. We're still waiting for him to regain consciousness following the surgery."

Nicole thanked Mindy and hurried to David's room. Once she found him, she scooted a chair over to the bed and picked up his hand, which was lying limp on the blanket. His nose was still swollen. His injured eye was now deep purple. Even so, he looked a little better than the last time she'd seen him. He'd been cleaned up, and some color had returned to his face. She started talking to him, saying anything that came into her head. She assured him that Steph would be home soon, safe and sound, and that he was going to be fine. "In a day or two," she said, "this nightmare will have passed."

David opened his good eye and looked at Nicole. Then he looked around the room and back at her. "What am I doing here?" he said.

"You passed out after you talked to the police. We had an ambulance bring you here."

He looked around again, confused. "Where's Steph?"

Just then a doctor stepped into the room holding a small electronic notebook. "Ah," he said to David. "I see you finally woke up. You had us a little worried there. Can you tell me your name?"

David hesitated, as if trying to remember. "David Stevenson," he finally said.

"Very good. Can you tell us where you are?"

"In the hospital."

"Good. And the date?"

David was silent for a good twenty seconds before he said. "I have no idea, Doc. And I've got one hell of a headache. My thoughts are all—" Again he stopped, groping for the word. "mixed up, like—" he paused. "Jumbled."

"This is to be expected. You've had brain surgery after a head injury. Do you remember how you got hurt?"

David looked confused. "Last thing I remember is when I went to sleep last night. Where's Steph?"

Nicole stood up and introduced herself to the doctor, who had yet to acknowledge her presence. "I'm David's fiancé's sister," she said. "Can we have a word?" She gestured toward the hallway, and the doctor followed her out.

"When I saw him this morning, a few hours after he was injured, he remembered every detail of my sister's abduction. Now he's even forgotten she's missing. Is that normal?"

"It's not unusual," the doctor said. "These memories may come back. Or maybe not. He took a significant blow to the head. In the next few days, weeks or maybe months, the aphasia will probably pass—"

"Aphasia?"

"Inability to recall words. You must have noticed how he was reaching for them. But he did summon them up, so I'd say it's probably a mild case. As for the confusion you mentioned, I think that will improve also. But I can't promise. There's still a lot we don't know about the brain. Some people go back to normal, while others—" he left the sentence unfinished, although his meaning was clear.

"Should I tell him what happened to my sister? It's sure to upset him."

"By all means, tell him. It may help jog loose some of those memories. But don't press him on what he remembers. These things take time, and it doesn't help to make him more anxious."

When Nicole returned to David, he again asked for Stephanie, looking genuinely worried.

Nicole sat down, took his hand, and told him what had happened.

"I think I knew this." His voice was shaky. "I mean, it doesn't seem real, more like something I dreamed." He stared at her intently and gulped. "How do I call the nurse? I think I'm going to be sick."

Nicole pushed the call button. Mindy appeared, located a kidney shaped bowl, and handed it to David. Instead of taking it, he broke down in great, heaving sobs. As he began to gain control of himself, he tried to speak.

"Sorry," Nicole said. "I didn't get what you said."

"This is all my fault. I know it is, if only I could remember. God, my head hurts. I can't think."

"None of this is your fault, David. Try to let it go." Nicole turned to the nurse, who was staring at David. She seemed as startled as Nicole by what he'd just said.

"Can you get him some pain meds and maybe a sedative?" Nicole said. "Aside from his headache, he's confused and agitated. This can't be good."

"I don't know," Mindy said. "They don't like to overmedicate patients with head injuries. I'll try to find his doctor and see if he'll prescribe something." She hurried away.

David went on talking, blaming himself for something he was unable to remember. As Nicole listened, she found David's words more and more disturbing. Arnault had mentioned the possibility that David might be involved in the kidnapping. What if it was true? In his present state, his defenses were down, as was his ability to dissemble. What If he was admitting to something he'd actually done. What if he really was mixed up in the kidnapping?

Nicole, who'd been holding his hand, dropped it.

Just then Mindy returned, carrying a syringe. She administered the shot, and it was only a moment or two before David was asleep. Unable to sit there any more with her terrible thoughts, Nicole got up and found her way back through the maze of corridors. After asking directions, she went over an indoor bridge she didn't remember crossing on her way in. From there, she located the parking structure and her car.

Back in her condo, she felt sick about Steph's disappearance, and David's confused rambling had upset her even more. She thought of Josh, her ex-fiancé. If this had happened a year ago, he'd have been here to comfort her. There were times she still missed him. For several months after she'd broken up with him and moved out, she'd sometimes come home to find him waiting in front of the apartment she was renting at the time. She'd let him in, they'd send out for food, and he'd end up spending the night. She'd hated herself for her weakness. She was preventing him from getting over her, which he had to do. He needed someone who wanted the same quiet life he did. Nicole knew that would never be her.

The last time she'd seen him, six months before, she hadn't let him in but had broken things off completely. As yet, she hadn't been interested in dating and had refused when friends attempted to fix her up. It seemed like too much work, too fraught with problems. And when she allowed herself to be honest about it, she had to admit she was still a little in love with Josh.

She thought of Arnault. There was definitely some chemistry between them. But she knew it would come to nothing. First came the ethics involved; he was a cop working on a case involving her sister. And even if they'd met under different circumstances, it would never work out. She'd been involved with a law enforcement type before and had learned her lesson. People who went into this line of work were married to the job. She wondered if she was overgeneralizing. There must be exceptions.

Still, she thought, it wasn't worth the risk of going through the pain of another breakup.

She glanced at her watch. It was almost seven o'clock in the evening, and she was beginning to feel hungry. When she looked in the refrigerator—empty of all but some eggs, a limp head of lettuce and a half loaf of bread in the freezer—she thought of the food she'd left at the market. Foraging through her cupboards, she located a can of tuna. She thought of defrosting the bread and making a grilled tuna sandwich but was too dispirited to make the effort. Instead, she pulled a box of crackers from the cupboard. She made herself a cup of tea, put the tuna and crackers on a plate, and placed this sorry excuse for a meal on a tray. She carried it into her study and turned on her computer. As she ate, she forced herself to focus on what she'd learned from Mr. and Mrs. Knowles.

She started going through property records of people who'd lived next to the Knowles's during the years Ashley would have been in her teens. It was a while before she found a family named Reese who were the Knowles's neighbors 12 years before. Alphonse had been close when he'd recollected the name as Meese. The Reeses had two daughters, Jessica and Melanie. Both had continued living with their parents past the age of 18 when they'd gotten jobs and established their own credit. That put them both on the database.

Nicole's next search focused on Jessica. Among the material that came up was a photo of the woman she knew as Ashley. She didn't look nearly as good as she had in recent pictures. Instead of being a glamorous blonde, Jessica was disheveled and devoid of makeup. her brown hair was falling out of a messy pony tail, as if she hadn't combed it that morning. She was scowling, and for good reason. There was a number under the photo, and it was a police mug shot.

Nicole read Jessica's records with great interest. The most recent entry was dated seven years ago: an outstanding arrest warrant for failing to report to her parole officer. A previous record showed she'd been granted early release from a five-year sentence in the New Mexico Women's Correctional Facility. She'd been convicted of fraud and theft, but the record gave no details of her crimes. Fortunately, the *New Mexico Enquirer* was indexed, and Nicole easily located an article that mentioned Jessica Reese as a member of a ring of crooks posing as caregivers for the elderly. They'd been convicted of bilking people out of their Social Security checks and emptying their checking accounts. Going back farther, Nicole came across New Mexico Youth Authority records from Jessica's teen years, but these were sealed.

Nicole made copies of the records and newspaper article to include with the report she was preparing for Robert Rexton. She couldn't give the information to the police. But she was pretty sure Rexton would hand it on to the detectives looking into his son's murder.

When she finished printing out Jessica Reese's records, she glanced at her watch. It was nine forty-five p.m. The ransom drop wasn't until eleven o'clock, and Griffith Park was only a little over six miles away. But the only route was through Hollywood. Even at night, traffic through the area was a nightmare. There was continuous gridlock around the iconic corner of Hollywood and Vine with its bright lights, garish neon signs, and celebrity billboards. After a moment's thought, she decided she might as well leave early. If people were still in the park, she'd wait in her car until they cleared out.

She grabbed her purse and the computer bag with the money Arnault had prepared for her. Only now did she remember she was supposed to include a note demanding proof of life. She went to the kitchen drawer where she kept a pen and pad of paper, tore off a sheet, and scrawled the message. After dropping it in the bag, she went down to her car.

Traffic was worse than she could have imagined. She didn't reach her destination until ten thirty, a half-hour before the appointed time. Centennial Park was a small, fenced off area just before the entrance to Griffith Park proper. She parked by the fence and took the path to her destination. Up ahead, the small recreational area of Centennial Park was brightly lit. This seemed puzzling at a time of night when few people would be out. Once inside the small park, she understood. The lights were there to discourage the homeless from using the area to sleep, but this hadn't worked. At least a dozen figures swathed in blankets and tarps lay on the grass, surrounding an enclave of small, round tents. She wondered if any of these people were the cops Arnault said would be here.

She headed for the only sizable tree, an enormous fir looming over a modest white stucco building. A sign in front welcomed her to the Centennial Park Senior Center. From where she stood, she couldn't see any hollow in the big tree's trunk. She glanced around at the sleeping figures. Then, satisfied no one was watching, she walked around the tree, pretending to be looking for something in the scrubby grass. On the other side, she spotted a sizable hollow in the trunk. She checked again to be sure she was unobserved before dropping the bag into the hole. Mission accomplished, she scurried back to her car, locked herself in, and headed home.

# EIGHT

THE NIGHT PASSED, and Stephanie slept like the dead. Only as she got up, shivering with cold, did she realize she was sick. Her dripping nose was now accompanied by a sore throat and a cough. Along with hunger, a solid mass of fear had settled in the pit of her stomach.

All her worries came flooding back. What had happened to David? Had these people hurt him? Killed him? Would she ever see him and Nicole again? She thought of the news stories about the recent kidnappings, the fact that two victims were missing. As far as she knew, they'd never been found. Had they been killed? Did these people plan to kill her, too?

A rattling sound at the top of the stairs caught her attention. It sounded as if something had been shoved through the slot in the door. Hoping for food, she hurried up as fast as she could. A tray sat on the shelf, holding the same offerings as the day before, a bowl of cereal and a mug. She ignored them and started banging on the door.

"It's freezing down here, and I'm starving. I need a solid meal and blankets and warm clothes. The light is burned out. Someone has to put in a new bulb." As an afterthought, she added, "And I need toilet paper."

There was no answer, although she could hear someone walking around. She pounded harder and shouted her requests again, this time in a succinct list: "Food, blankets, clothes, light bulb, toilet paper. Please!!"

The footsteps stopped, but there was still no response. She went back down the stairs with the cup and bowl and got back in bed. Swaddled in her blanket, she took a sip of what was in the mug, expecting coffee. This time it was tea, bitter and barely warm, as if it had sat out, steeping, for a good, long while. She drank it anyway. She took a spoonful of cereal and almost spit it out. The milk had gone sour. It had probably been left unrefrigerated overnight. Famished, she forced herself to eat it, despite the taste. This might be the only meal she'd get today.

Footsteps started up again. Suddenly the door at the top of the stairs opened. A figure—just a silhouette in black—tossed a bundle down the stairs and closed the door. The whole process had taken only seconds, too quick for her to get a look at who it was.

It was obvious that this person was trying to avoid being seen. Her captors were afraid she'd be able to identify them. She found this slightly reassuring. It suggested they meant to release her. If they planned to kill her, they wouldn't care whether she saw them or not.

The objects he'd tossed into the basement dropped to the floor with barely a sound. She got up to take a look. To her surprise, the bundle included almost everything she'd requested. There were two blankets, men's sweatpants, a sweater, and a roll of toilet paper. Missing were the lightbulb and food. The blankets were full of dust and the clothes stank of sweat and a musky, masculine odor that didn't bear thinking about. There were no socks, shoes, or slippers, nothing to cover her feet. That would be her next request.

Despite the way the clothes smelled, she was so cold that she quickly put them on. She had to make adjustments. The sweater was huge and had holes in the elbows. These didn't matter since she had to fold up her sleeves several times to free her hands. The pant legs had to be rolled up as well, and the waist was too loose, even with the cord pulled as tight as it would go.

As soon as she stood up, the pants slipped down around her hips and were in danger of falling down. She tucked the bulky sweater inside, and the added girth stabilized the pants. Feeling a bit warmer, she folded the blankets. She was just setting them on the bed when she heard the flap open and something else slid onto the shelf.

She hurried up again to find a large flashlight sitting there. She'd been hoping for food, but was glad to get the flashlight. Its beam was strong, which meant the batteries were fresh. She waved it around the basement for her first good look at her surroundings. The place was filthy; no wonder it smelled. The walls were covered with cobwebs, the floor splotched with stains of varying darkness and scattered rat droppings. It really did resemble a dungeon. On the other hand, there were no instruments of torture or indication that anyone else had been held prisoner here.

She decided to give the basement a thorough exploration. If there was a way out besides the locked door at the head of the stairs, she was determined to find it. Without the flashlight, it had been too dark for her to see under the stairs or into the crawl space. The low hum of a motor had stirred her curiosity. Was a generator being charged? Did home generators need charging? She had no idea.

The sound was coming from under the stairs. Focusing the beam of her flashlight into the darkness, she noticed a huge spider web across the entry to the space. Unlike most, Stephanie wasn't afraid of spiders. At age eight, she'd fallen under the spell of *Charlotte's Web* and had become fascinated with arachnids. She'd read every book she could find about them. She loved closeups of their faces with their multiple pairs of eyes and, most especially, the way they could sail on a breeze to spin their webs across wide spaces. To her, they were magical.

Stephanie had gone through a phase of catching spiders and keeping them in jars with holes carefully punctured in the tops. She'd even given the spiders names, which she wrote on the jars with a marker. But when she noticed their high mortality rate, she realized these creatures didn't do well in captivity, and she stopped trying to make pets of them. Even as an adult, she'd never step on a spider she found inside. Instead, she'd capture it in a glass, slip a piece of cardboard under it, and release it outdoors.

She realized it would be easy to break the web apart with her flashlight, but she hesitated. From her study of spiders, she knew that the brown recluse, the country's most venomous arachnid, was a Southern California native that hung out in dark basements. There was good reason to think that the creator of this giant web might well be a brown recluse. She wasn't going to touch the web unless she could figure out a way protect herself from a spider bite.

Stepping back, she used the flashlight to see what else was under there. The area held two old appliances. One was a refrigerator with its plug lying on the floor. Next to it was what looked like an old-fashioned deep freezer, like the one her parents kept in their garage. This, she decided, was the source of the hum. She wondered what was in it.

Under the bottom steps, the flashlight's beam picked up a glint of something shiny. She bent down to get a better look. It was a screwdriver with a yellow plastic handle, and it appeared to be new. Someone must have put it down while working on something down here. It had rolled under the steps and been forgotten.

The screwdriver with its sharp, chiseled end could make a formidable weapon. She tried to picture herself sticking it in the eye of one of her captors. The idea made her shudder, and she knew she'd never be able to do such a thing. Even so, she decided to retrieve the tool and stash it somewhere handy in case she found a use for it. Although the screwdriver was nowhere near the huge web, it was well out of reach. She'd have to crawl part way under the steps to get it. She got down on her hands and knees, took a deep breath and—not allowing herself to think about it—pushed her head and shoulders under the steps.

Almost immediately, a web she hadn't seen caught in her hair. She felt, or imagined she felt, something crawling on her neck. She bumped her head backing out. Ignoring the pain, she used her sleeve to wipe as much of the web out of her hair as possible. The tingling sensation on her neck had disappeared, and she chalked it up to imagination. She checked the screwdriver's position again, then turned the flashlight off to conserve the battery and put it down. Inching along on her belly, she kept her head down so she wouldn't bang it again. This time she was able to grab the screwdriver and wriggle back out. She went directly into the bathroom to look in the mirror and make sure she wasn't covered with spider webs.

When she saw her reflection, she let out a scream. Sitting on her sleeve was an inch-long brown spider with the identifying outline of a fiddle on its back. Not knowing what else to do, she used the flashlight to shove it off. The spider dropped to the floor and lay still. Only then did she realize it was dead and probably had been dead before it fell on her. She used toilet paper to pick it up and drop it in the toilet.

Looking around for a place to hide the screwdriver, she ended up pushing it between the slats that covered the crawl space. She left the business end of the screwdriver sticking out so she could easily grab it. Then she checked from different angles to make sure it couldn't be seen.

Next, she turned her attention to the crawlspace. The slats covering the opening were brittle, and it was easy to break some off to get a better look. She slowly moved the flashlight around. Now she could see that the vent admitting light was closer than she'd thought—ten feet at most. It was too small for anything but insects and rodents to get through. She waved the light around once more, wondering how many of the spider's relatives might be hiding there. Even though she didn't see any webs on the route to the vent, she doubted it was worth crawling through the dirt to get a look outside. Perhaps the view would allow her to figure out where the house was situated. If there were neighbors nearby, she could call for help, or maybe she'd see something that would aid her escape. But these possibilities seemed unlikely.

Just then, Stephanie heard a door slam above. Was he leaving? She dashed up the stairs and pounded on the door. "I'm hungry! Don't leave me here without more food!"

There was no answer, and she was certain he was gone. As she started back downstairs, she was overwhelmed by fatigue. All at once she understood why she was so sleepy. She was being drugged. Most likely they'd put it in the drinks, the coffee and lukewarm tea. She vowed not to drink anything else they brought her, no matter how tempting. She dragged herself back to the bed and fell asleep.

She opened her eyes sometime later, woken by footsteps on the floor above. It went quiet for what seemed like a long time, although her watch said only 20 minutes had passed. She hadn't heard the front door close, so she figured he must still be up there. This time he didn't open the door, but the rattling meant he was using the slot to deliver something. More food, she thought, dashing up the stairs to get a look. There was a carton of coffee, purchased from a café, the kind she bought when she was expecting a crowd. It would stay hot for several hours. Next to it stood a chipped ceramic mug. Tempting as the coffee might be, she resisted pouring herself a cup. She had no doubt it was drugged, and she needed to stay alert so she could figure a way out.

Also sitting on the tray was a stack of three aluminum-foil containers of frozen meals that had been heated. She was so hungry that the food, which she normally would have refused, smelled delicious. She tried to pick one up, but the container burned her fingers. She pulled the long sleeves of her sweatshirt over her hands. The thick fabric made a perfect potholder. She carried the meals downstairs, sat on the bed, and put one on her lap. When she peeled back the foil cover, she saw the meal was turkey meatloaf, mashed potatoes, and mixed vegetables. Only now did she realize she didn't have an eating utensil. She'd left the spoon in the cereal bowl when she'd taken it up to the shelf that morning. She wasn't going to ask for a knife and fork. She'd have to wait until the food cooled so she could use her fingers. At that moment, she heard the front door slam and a car start up. She was alone again.

Stephanie ate all three meals, one after the other. She'd been right about her beverages being drugged. By avoiding the coffee they'd brought this morning, she was wide awake. On the other hand, she was so scared and agitated that she wondered if she'd be better off asleep. But no. She had to stay alert, watching and waiting for a chance to escape.

She wandered aimlessly around the basement but found nothing she hadn't already noticed. She lay down, her mind racing. Would she get out of this place alive? If not, who would mourn her? Her parents were dead. The only family she had was Nicole. As she thought about her sister, she pictured Nicole worrying, using her detective skills in an attempt to find out what had happened. She teared up as she imagined Nicole's reaction when she found out her little sister was dead. David would be sad, too. Very sad, she supposed. But he'd get over it and find someone else. In the past week, she'd begun to have doubts about the marriage they were about to embark on. Maybe it was just bridal jitters, but she'd been overcome with the urge to postpone it.

She felt that David was asking too much of her too soon. He wanted a family and didn't want to wait long before starting it. But how could she make the leap from being a free spirit to what David expected her to become: a married woman and, in short order, a mother. She had a hard time picturing this transformation.

She'd told David about her feelings the night before. He'd been shocked, disbelieving, pointing out that, only a few days ago, she'd been as enthusiastic about the wedding as he was. Without thinking or bothering to be tactful, she'd told him she was having doubts about her feelings for him. Almost as soon as the words were out, she regretted them.

"Why did you accept my proposal if you don't want to marry me?" David said.

"I didn't mean that," she said. "I just need more time."

"More time for what?" he'd said. "Squandering your life on losers like the ones you used to go out with? Taking odd jobs that don't pay a living wage?" Once he got started, he grew angrier and said some pretty mean things about the direction of her life.

By now, she was angry, too. "Get out!" she'd yelled, even though they were at his place, and she was the one who should have left. Instead, David had taken his pillow, gotten blankets from the linen closet, and decamped to the living room couch.

Her cough was getting worse, as was her sore throat, and she'd begun to feel feverish. She got up from the bed, helped herself to a wad of toilet paper to blow her nose, and paced around, her thoughts in a jumble. She loved David; she really did, but she was stung by the things he'd said. He had a point about her past decisions, but what gave him the right to make her feel so small? She couldn't help it if she needed to postpone the wedding. She just wasn't ready—not until she got her act together.

That was another of her problems. What was her act? She didn't know. She'd dropped out of college after two years. In the eight years since, she'd steadfastly refused to join the conventional workforce. Instead, she'd picked up odd jobs: some computer work, like setting up websites for old ladies who wanted to show off their dogs, cats, horses and, once, a small herd of llamas. She haunted community centers, looking for notices put up by people who needed tech support, setting up computers and learning how to use them. She'd also done pet sitting, house sitting, dog walking. She'd even worked for a telephone-sex operation, which she'd found highly entertaining. It was also the best-paid freelance job she'd ever had. She'd quit when the company that employed her switched to video chats and expected her to answer calls wearing sexy lingerie.

When one set of jobs dried up, she'd beat the bushes for more. Sometimes she'd get so overloaded that she'd be putting in ten- and twelve-hour days. Even then, these part-time, temporary jobs provided only a marginal living. Without Nicole's help, there were months when Steph wouldn't have been able to make the rent.

Having a sister like Nicole created its own set of problems. Steph felt as if she was always being unfavorably compared with her sister. It wasn't Nicole's fault. Sure, they had an occasional dust-up. But Nicole was always willing to help Steph out, provide emotional support, and steer her away from some of her bad decisions. But other people were always making comparisons. As far back as Steph could remember, it had been tough following in her sister's footsteps. Nicole, highly motivated in school, got straight As. She was popular and pretty in a sweet, dimpled way that disguised her determination and competence.

Teachers who'd had Nicole were initially delighted to get Steph. But she sensed that they expected a carbon copy of her older sister, and how could Steph live up to that? She'd never liked school, and she hated homework. More than that, she was always testing the rules and getting into trouble. Steph wondered if she'd taken the easy way out by refusing to compete with Nicole. Or was her nonconformist streak and acting-out another form of sibling rivalry? If she couldn't be like Nicole, she'd excel at being the opposite, an irresponsible kook.

Tired of thinking about it, she made another round of the basement, trying to come up with an escape plan. There was no way out except through the door at the top of the stairs. What would Nicole do, she asked herself. Steph gazed up at the door. Only one man seemed to come each time, although she was sure more had to be involved in order to overpower David and carry her off. She tried to imagine a ruse that would lure the man downstairs. But even if she succeeded, she'd need a way to disable him or tie him up before she could escape.

It seemed hopeless. Besides, there was the question of the house's location. Was it in L.A. or in some remote area where it would be impossible to find help or walk away?

She thought about her life again, looking back with deep regret. What if this basement was the end of the line, and she was going to die here? What would her life have added up to? Just a series of mindless good times and a remarkable lack of accomplishments.

These thoughts reduced her to tears. She lay down again and cried until she noticed, with a start, that it was already dark. That meant no one was coming back with food until tomorrow. She regretted eating all three meals at once. Now she was hungrier than ever. With a sick and sorry heart, she lay down on the bed and tried in vain to sleep.

# NINE

NICOLE ENCOUNTERED EVEN WORSE traffic after leaving the ransom in Centennial Park. In addition to tourists milling around Hollywood's star-studded sidewalks, Madame Tussauds, and Grauman's Chinese Theater, long lines of young people were waiting to get into clubs. Every car seemed to be changing lanes, slowing whenever it looked as if a parking spot might open up. It was well past midnight before she got home.

She was exhausted from the strain of the day and sick with worry. Despite her fatigue, she was too keyed up to sleep. Not knowing what else to do with herself, she got ready for bed. As Arnault had suggested, she set the burner phone next to her cell on her night table, checking to be sure they were both charging. She spent the night tossing and turning with worries that turned uglier with each passing hour. She would have sworn she hadn't slept. But she must have dropped off because the ringing of the burner phone woke her at six o'clock. Her heart was pounding as she picked it up.

"They didn't show," Arnault said. "We have to talk."

"What do you mean? No one picked up the money? What about Steph? Do you think something—" her voice broke, and she had to swallow hard before she could go on. "Has something happened to her?"

"All it means," he said, "is that they figured out we were there. They want that money and keeping your sister safe is the only way they're going to get it. But I want to meet with you before work so we can talk. Is there a coffee shop in your office building?"

"On the first floor. You don't have to go through security to get in."

"Great. I'll meet you there at eight o'clock."

Nicole got to the coffee shop fifteen minutes early. Arnault was already there, drinking coffee in one of the booths. She slid in across from him. "So, what now?" she said.

"We'll have to wait until you hear from them again. What I'm wondering—" he stopped. A waitress was standing by the table, waiting for their attention. They both ordered, Nicole without looking at the menu.

When the waitress was gone, Arnault went on. "I'm wondering how they found out we were there. Did you tell anyone you'd called the police?"

"Of course not." She thought for a moment. "Well, David knew, of course. He was there when I made the call. But he had to have surgery yesterday because of the head injury. When I visited him late in the day, he had no memory of anything that happened after they went to bed that night. I had to break the news of Steph's kidnapping.

"In any case, he wouldn't have told anyone. He was terrified because the kidnappers swore they'd kill Steph if he called the police. He wanted to use a private hostage negotiation firm. He felt they'd be more focused on working directly with the kidnappers by paying the ransom and getting Steph back home without delay."

Arnault raised an eyebrow. "Is that what he said? That he

wanted the ransom paid but wasn't interested in catching the perps?"

Despite her own suspicions, Nicole didn't like what he was suggesting. "No. I mean yes," she said. "But only because he was afraid of what might happen to Steph if we called the police."

"For all your smarts, you're pretty naïve," Arnault said. "As I said before, Stevenson could have had someone beat him up to make him look like a victim when he's actually one of the perpetrators."

Nicole was silent, remembering how David had believed he was somehow responsible for Steph's disappearance. At first, this had alarmed her, making her wonder if he really was involved. Now she was inclined to think that David was simply confused. His failure to stop the intruders made him feel guilty. He wasn't able to sort out his emotions because he had no recollection of the break-in. Nicole was glad she'd had Sue intervene so the police couldn't continue questioning him. In his current state, who knew what they could get him to confess to?

"OK. Go on," Arnault said. "Who else knew?"

"My lawyer, Sue Price. She's the one I called when David asked for an attorney."

"How long have you known Ms. Price?"

"About three years. She's a good friend, as well as my attorney. I'd trust her with my life. Other than that," she shook her head. She explained that she'd spent the day pretending nothing was wrong. "So, what's next?"

"Continue to go about your life as you normally would. The kidnappers will contact you with instructions for another drop. And don't be surprised if they ask for more on the second go. That's par for the course. Meanwhile, find time today to return to the park and pick up the bag with the ransom." He got out his card and jotted something on the back. "I don't think you're in any danger, but I want a plainclothesman to keep an eye on you when you go out there. Call this number before you leave."

The waitress was back, placing their food on the table. Nicole nibbled at her scrambled eggs and toast, while Arnault wolfed down a full breakfast of eggs over easy, sausages, and blueberry pancakes.

"Let me know when you hear from them." Arnault gazed into her eyes with what looked like genuine sympathy. "I know how worried and upset you are. But I promise we're doing everything possible to get Stephanie home safe. We have a crack team working on this, and we have some solid leads." He stood, got out his wallet, and tossed a few bills on the table. "That should take care of my share. I've got to go."

As he was walking away, Nicole glanced through the glass partition into the building's lobby. Joanne, just arriving at work, was staring at her. Nicole waved, put down enough money to cover her share of the meal, and hurried into the lobby.

"So, you met that hot techy for breakfast. Fast work," Joanne gave a smile. "Good for you. You've seemed a little blue lately. You need to start dating again."

Nicole simply nodded. Maybe it was best Joanne thought Arnault was a romantic interest. That would provide an excuse if he needed to come by again.

By lunchtime, Nicole still hadn't heard from the kidnappers. Her anxiety had built to the point that she couldn't sit in her office any longer. Maybe some fresh air would help. She made sure both the burner phone and her cell were in her purse and set her office phone to call forwarding. On her way out of the building, she picked up a turkey sandwich from the deli case in the coffee shop in case she got hungry. Once on her way, she headed briskly along Wilshire Boulevard toward the county museum.

After a block or two, she had the feeling she was being watched. She stopped next to one of the highrises, got out her makeup mirror, and angled it to see if anyone was following her. A man in a Dodger's T-shirt and khakis, half a block behind, had stopped and seemed to be looking in her direction, although it was hard to be sure. She started walking again, faster now, and casually glanced around. He was on the move again, walking at the same clip she was. She wondered if he was with the police. Had Arnault sent him to make sure she wasn't meeting with the kidnappers on her own? She thought of a possibility she liked even less, that this might be one of the kidnappers with who-knew-what in mind.

When she got to the La Brea Tar Pits, the place was unusually crowded. It took a moment for her to realize why. The park had a new feature that was getting a lot of publicity. Today, it had attracted a crowd that made it the perfect place to hide while she figured out how to lose the man following her.

She hurried into the middle of the gathering. There she paused, standing on tiptoe to see past the people gathered at the edge of the black pond where tar slowly undulated with bubbles of oily gas.

At that moment, an enormous creature—a life-like tyrannosaurus rex—emerged from the goo. His skin must have had a special coating because the tar slid off him as he rose. Once he was all the way out of the dark pond, he stood erect, gazing around, as if deciding which of the spectators to have for lunch. Even though it was only a robot, it was frighteningly realistic, as if the curators had raided *Jurassic Park*. Suddenly, the dinosaur let out a roar and lunged toward a group of tourists. Instinctively, the crowd moved back, and a small boy let out a shriek, hiding in his mother's skirt. People around Nicole laughed nervously, keeping it down as if afraid of attracting the creature's attention.

After perhaps thirty seconds, the robot began sinking back into the tar, struggling as if a powerful force were sucking it under. The whole spectacle took just a few minutes. For that brief time, it took Nicole's mind off Steph and the stranger. Once the creature disappeared under the muck and the crowd began to disburse, Nicole looked around for an escape route. Behind the tar pit's museum, she spotted a path lined with tall shrubs. She was pretty sure it led to the park's rear entrance, one street north, and would allow her to return to her building without encountering her shadow. She hurried toward it. She reached the side street and walked quickly back to work, her mind buzzing with Stephanie's plight, David's injury, the question of what would happen next, and when, if, and how the kidnappers would get in touch. Now she had a new worry: Who was following her and why?

As soon as she got back to her office, she called Arnault. "Do you have someone following me?"

"Now, why would we be following you?" he said.

"To make sure I don't make a private arrangement to pay the kidnappers without police involvement."

"Did you actually see someone following you?" he said.

"I did, and I was worried it might be one of the kidnappers. Then I thought maybe you were responsible."

"Absolutely not," he said. "We aren't following you."

"Would you tell me if you were?"

"No."

She gave a laugh. "All right, then. I take it you have been following me."

"I will say this. Now that you've told me you're being followed, you can be sure we'll be keeping an eye on you. As for making a private arrangement with these criminals, I can see it might be tempting. But it would be a terrible mistake. Listen, I can't talk now. Assuming the kidnappers don't call this afternoon demanding a drop tonight, let's meet after work so I can fully explain the downside of paying ransom directly."

Nicole thought of the long evening ahead. She was free, all right. "Sure," she said.

"There's a place in West Hollywood, Bernini's," he said. "I could meet you there at seven thirty. You need directions?"

"No, I'll find it. Bernini's," she repeated. "I'll see you at seven thirty."

After they hung up, she considered what he'd said. She couldn't help thinking there must be a way to reach a deal with the kidnappers without getting killed. All these people wanted was the money. Still, the thought of having someone to spend the evening with was comforting. She wouldn't have to sit home alone, waiting to hear from the kidnappers.

A moment later, Nicole found herself typing "Arnault, Greg" into her computer. Under normal circumstances, she was insatiably curious about everyone who came into her life. If she hadn't been so upset about Steph, she would have checked out Arnault when she first met him.

When his name came up, she learned he was thirty-five and had never been married. He was a native Angeleno who'd attended local public schools and then her own alma mater, UCLA. In fact, they'd both been there at the same time. It wasn't surprising she'd never encountered him. The school had more than thirty thousand undergraduates. Arnault had earned a B.A. in art history, then completed his MFA. He'd been teaching at Newhall Community College, when he quit to join the police force.

Nicole wondered what had happened to make him change direction so completely. He'd been a beat cop for a couple of years before earning several promotions that landed him on the elite Robbery and Homicide squad.

When she finished reading about Arnault, she thought of David and put in a call to the hospital. They connected her to his room, and he picked up.

"Hey," he said. "What's going on with Steph? Have you gotten the money to the kidnappers yet?" He sounded more clear-headed than he had earlier.

"David," she said. "We can't discuss this on the phone. You never know who might be listening. Everything's going according to plan. I just have to wire them the money. It's all working out. Okay?"

"Yeah. But will you call me when the money is wired? I'm just lying here, going crazy. I don't mean to be a whiner, but—God,

I'm so worried about her."

"I know. But I'm sure it's going to be okay. I'm following the kidnappers' directions, understand? We should have her home in a day or two."

"Thanks," David's voice was thick, as if he were crying. "Thank you, Nicole. I knew I could count on you."

After they hung up, Nicole felt guilty that she hadn't called David earlier. In the crush of events, her thoughts had been elsewhere.

She spent the rest of the afternoon finishing up her report on Ashley for Rexton. She was relieved that she'd managed to track down more of Ashley's past, confirm that Ashley was an identity assumed by someone named Jessica Reese, and furnish proof that Jessica was a criminal. She couldn't hand the report over to the police because of confidentiality rules. But she was sure Rexton would. Maybe that would get the police focused on locating Ashley.

She showed the report to Jerry, who leaned back in his chair and read it while she waited. "Great detective work," he said. "Go ahead and send it to Rexton."

It was three in the afternoon when she emailed the report. She was looking over her next assignment when someone tapped on her office door.

"Come in," she said.

It was Joanne. "You got a minute?"

"Of course," Nicole said. "What's up?"

Joanne sat down and studied Nicole before she spoke. "That's exactly what I was going to ask you. Are you going to tell me what's going on? Anyone can see you're under a lot of stress. At first I thought it had something to do with techie boy, like you were lovesick or something. But I can see it's more serious than that. Come on," she said. "I'm your friend. Maybe I can help."

Nicole looked away. It was tempting to pour out the whole story to Joanne. But what would that accomplish? It wouldn't lighten her burden, nor could Joanne do anything to help. This would be one more person in the loop, worrying about Steph and asking for updates.

Nicole was quiet, searching around for an explanation that would sound convincing. Finally, she said, "Stephanie's not well, and they're doing a bunch of tests. I've been worried, that's all."

"Oh, I'm sorry to hear it," Joanne said. "Keep me posted, okay?" But her expression suggested she wasn't buying it. More tellingly, she didn't ask questions about the nature of Steph's illness, something she'd normally have done.

At four o'clock., Nicole shut down her computer and called the number on the card Arnault had given her. She spoke to a woman who said she'd send an unmarked car to Centennial Park immediately. With this out of the way, Nicole left for the long drive to retrieve the bundle of phony cash. It wasn't until close to six thirty that she pulled into her parking spot in her condo's garage. She stopped the elevator on the first floor to check her mailbox for a note or notice of a delivery. But there was nothing.

# TEN

STEPHANIE DOZED FITFULLY. She woke a little later, feeling worse than before. In addition to her other miseries, her chest hurt from coughing. It was dark, and her watch said seven o'clock, too late for any of her captors to return with more food.

She had an idea. Maybe she could use the screwdriver to get the door unlocked. She climbed the stairs again, using the flashlight to guide her. She didn't really think it would work, but it was worth a try.

She was almost at the top when she noticed that the third step down was different from the others, lighter in color and much more solid when she put her weight on it. It looked new. The original step must have broken and been replaced with this one. Earlier, she'd noticed that the steps were rickety and buckled slightly under her weight. She wondered if she could choose one and jump on it enough to weaken it. This would be tricky. She wouldn't want to actually break the step, just get it to the point where it would collapse under the next person's weight. The bigger problem would be figuring out how to lure one of the men downstairs. She'd get to that later.

She went back to the bottom of the stairs and worked her way up, training the flashlight under each step to find the most promising candidate. As she inspected them, she understood why they were in such bad shape. They'd been undermined by termites and dry rot.

When she reached the one that had been replaced, she saw that—unlike the others—it was fastened with screws to something underneath. Leaning down to inspect it, she saw that someone had gone to a lot of trouble to shore it up. A metal bar, attached to the wall, ran all the way across the bottom. Attached to the bar were three one-inch blocks of wood that supported the step from back to front. The wood pieces were held in place by the screws she'd noticed on top of the step. This explained how the screwdriver had ended up under the stairs. Whoever had repaired this step must have set the screwdriver down. It had rolled off, fallen to the floor, and been forgotten.

She went to work. Sitting two steps above the newly installed one, she set about removing the screws. There were six of them, screwed in so tight it took enormous effort to get each to start turning. Once the step was loose, she slid it slightly forward so there wasn't a gap between the loose step and the one above. She pressed down with her hand to see what would happen. The step slid forward onto the one below. She put it back and, tightly gripping the handrail, placed her foot on the loosened step, bearing down. This time it flew out from under her, landing halfway down the stairs. Steph was pleased that she, with so little mechanical ability, had been able to set up a booby trap. She put the step back, making sure it would slide out easily.

She went downstairs and returned the screwdriver to its hiding place. She told herself that by morning, when someone showed up to feed her, she'd have thought of a way to get her captor to come downstairs. A half hour later, she was surprised to hear someone enter the house. She wondered if he might be bringing more food. But his footsteps didn't come near the basement door. Apparently he'd come to pick up something or drop it off. Only a few minutes passed before she heard him head back in the direction he'd entered. He was leaving, and she had to stop him. She started beating on the door, yelling the first thing that came into her head. "Help! A pipe broke down here, and it's flooding the basement."

There was a pause before she heard footsteps hurrying in her direction. The basement door opened just enough for the man to shine a flashlight in. It found her halfway down the steps, its glare almost blinding her. Then the light moved around the basement floor.

"You're lying," The man sounded young—early twenties, perhaps. "I don't see any water. The floor isn't even wet."

"That's because the basement floor isn't level," she said. "Water is pooling under the stairs. A refrigerator or something is plugged in under there. Before, I could hear it running. Now it's gone quiet."

"Shit!" The man immediately started down the stairs. The loose step worked just as she'd hoped, flying out from beneath his foot. Waving his arms wildly, he tried to recover his balance. With nothing to step back on, he tumbled to the bottom, screaming all the way.

He was quiet so long that Stephanie wondered if the fall had killed him. Then he started to moan, soon switching to loud complaints. "My arm! Oh, my God, it's broke! Help! It's killing me!" Before long, his cries were interspersed with sobs.

He'd landed several feet from the stairs. Stephanie walked around him and started up to the open door. She stopped halfway, looking down at him. He was clearly in agony. Despite everything, she found herself feeling sorry for him. She couldn't do anything to help him. But she promised herself that, as soon as she got away, she'd call 911 to get an ambulance, as well as the police, out here to pick him up. This decided, she hurried up the stairs, locked the basement door, and walked out of the house. But before she'd taken more than a few steps, she heard a car door slam, echoed by a second slam a moment later. She froze when she saw that two men had gotten out of a car parked on the street above and were starting toward her. She could only guess that all three men had arrived together, but only one of them had gone into the house while the others waited.

She turned right and started running, only to be stopped at the edge of the property by a cyclone fence hidden behind overgrown shrubs. She headed in the other direction, but the men were waiting, blocking her path. They grabbed her, each by an arm, and dragged her back in the house. She had no doubt these were partners of the man she'd left on the basement floor. One was medium height with a muscular build and buzz haircut. The other was tall and thin, dressed in a suit and tie.

"Great," said Muscles. "Now she's seen us and can identify us."

"So what?" said the guy in the suit. "By the time the police find her, we'll be long gone."

"If you believe that, you're even dumber than I thought. Let's see what's happened to Matt. I thought he was taking too long in there. She must have done something to him."

By now they were at the door to the basement, which Muscles unlocked. A moment later, he pulled a gun out of his pocket and pointed it at Stephanie. "You lead the way. We'll follow." The guy in the suit focused his flashlight on the stairs to guide them. Steph went down, taking care to skip over the missing step. The two men did the same.

The one called Matt, who'd fallen downstairs, was still moaning, letting out an occasional sob. Muscles ran ahead and bent over him. They were talking when the guy in the suit, still holding onto Stephanie, joined them.

"She found a way to loosen that new step," Muscles said. "He came down here because she told him it was flooded under the stairs, and the freezer went off. Well, don't just stand there."

Muscles sounded profoundly exasperated. "Go and look. I'll hold onto her." None too gently, he grabbed Stephanie's arm.

It wasn't long before the guy in the suit was back. His hair and shoulders were draped in spiderwebs, which he was attempting to brush off. "There isn't any flood. The freezer is running fine. It was a trick."

Muscles pulled Stephanie toward the staircase. "Okay, bitch. I'm going to throw you down the stairs and see how you like it."

The guy in the suit put a hand on Muscle's shoulder. "Look, Ry—" he stopped himself, but it was easy to figure out Muscle's name was Ryan. "We're not to hurt her in any way. She's our collateral, remember? Our job is to make sure nothing happens to her so we can collect the ransom. You understand that, right?"

Ryan let go of Stephanie. "Just as long as I get to shoot her after the ransom is paid."

"Nobody's shooting anyone." Now the guy in the suit sounded out of patience.

"Let's tie her up so she doesn't cause any more trouble," Ryan said.

"How am I supposed to get the food you leave or use the bathroom if I'm tied up?" Stephanie interjected.

"That's easy," Ryan said. "We'll get you a bucket and stop feeding you. We can't trust you running around loose down here. Who knows what you'll pull next."

"Tying her up will just complicate things," the guy in the suit said. "We'll nail the door shut after we lock it and be extra careful whenever we open it. Right now we've got to take Matt to Emergency. He's in a lot of pain."

They ordered Stephanie to sit in a far corner while they brought Matt upstairs. He was no lightweight, and he yelled in pain as they half dragged, half carried him up.

Stephanie was so hungry that her stomach was growling, but she didn't dare ask for food. She'd been lucky not to get thrown down the stairs or tied up. The last thing she wanted was to call attention to herself.

She felt hopeless, trapped. Now that she'd seen the faces of all three men, they'd never let her go.

# ELEVEN

WITH ONLY FORTY-FIVE MINUTES before she was to meet Arnault at Bernini's, Nicole rushed around freshening up, hot-rollering her hair, and repairing her makeup. The whole time she kept telling herself how silly this was. With all that was going on, was she really trying to pretty herself up for Arnault? God, what a mess she was.

The only reason they were meeting was so he could explain the downside of paying the kidnappers on her own, without help from the police. As she considered this, she couldn't help thinking there must be a way to reach a deal with the men who'd taken Steph without anyone getting hurt. All these people wanted was money, money she didn't care about.

Fighting her way through rush-hour traffic, she was twenty minutes late getting to the restaurant. Bernini's turned out to be a tiny wine bar in West Hollywood. It was pretty: candles on the tables, white tablecloths, pink napkins, and a handsome bar backed by tilted mirrors that reflected the restaurant's interior at interesting angles. Arnault was in a small booth at the very back, nursing a glass of red wine. She slid in opposite him. He greeted her, then held up his hand to summon the waiter. She ordered pinot grigio.

After Nicole's wine was delivered, Arnault said, "I'm going to explain about hostage negotiations, and then we're closing the subject. Consider tonight a—" he hesitated—"a way of taking your mind off what you're going through."

"Isn't it against police regulations to fraternize with 'civilians' involved in a case you're investigating?"

"A lot of things are against regulations," he said, taking a sip of his wine. "Like drinking on duty."

"Are you on duty?"

"No. That's my point. What I do on my own time—within reason—is nobody's business. Now, about making a private arrangement with these criminals. Here's what would happen: They'd insist you deliver the ransom to a secluded location, then they'd take you, too. They'd force you to go to your bank and wire the rest of your money to an offshore account they've set up or change it into funny money on the web. After that, they'd have every reason to get rid of you and your sister. They're already responsible for the death of Brad Rexton, possibly Ashley and the other missing woman. If they're clever enough—which I doubt, by the way—we might never find out what became of you.

"As for hiring crisis intervention experts or a private security firm—no way they have the expertise we do. You'd be amazed at the amount of experience and advanced technology at our disposal for such cases.

"That's all I have to say about this," he said. "Subject closed."

"I have one more question," she said. "What about David? Is he still a suspect?"

Arnault looked down at the table for a moment and then back at her. "I'm not supposed to discuss the case with you. You know that, right?"

"I know. But still . . . "

"I'll say this. He does have alibis for the nights of the first two abductions."

"Do I hear a 'but' in there?"

He took a deep breath. "We're not ruling anybody out just yet. Personally, I don't think he had anything to do with it."

"That's a relief," she said. "Because I know he didn't. He's a really good guy."

"Change of subject," he said. "Let's talk about you. What made you decide to go into private investigation?"

"I don't feel like talking about myself right now," Nicole said. "But I do have a question for you."

"Go ahead." He smiled and relaxed back in his seat.

"I did a background check on you and—"

He chuckled. "Of course, you did. I'd be disappointed in you if you hadn't."

She smiled at him, and they studied each other for a long moment. Finally, Nicole said, "So why did you go into police work? You got an MFA from UCLA and were teaching art history at Newhall Community College. That's not the usual path into law enforcement."

He withdrew his gaze and looked away, absentmindedly twirling his wineglass. He seemed to be considering what to say, or perhaps whether he wanted to say anything at all. He shifted in his seat and turned back to her. "You're right. Most people wouldn't switch from a comfortable perch teaching art history to work as a rookie cop. But shit happens and, as they say, life is full of detours. For one thing, I was always interested in crime and law enforcement. As an undergrad, I took a number of classes that dealt with criminal justice. But I never thought of it as a career.

"About five years ago, I was involved with a woman. After a few months, we moved in together and were talking about marriage. One night, she didn't come home from teaching an evening class. I called everyone we knew. No one had seen her after she'd left her classroom. I went to bed not knowing what to think.

"We'd had a fight that day, and I thought she might be staying with a friend to punish me or even hooking up with the guy we'd had the fight about. She said he was just a friend. I'm not the jealous type, but I had reason to believe it was more than that. I said some things I deeply regret, especially since those were the last words I ever spoke to her."

He took another sip of wine. "The next morning, when I turned on the news, I learned that a woman had been raped and murdered in one of the campus parking structures. At first, I told myself it couldn't be Aline. She always rode her bike to class, so what would she be doing in a parking structure? Later I learned someone had grabbed her, thrown her into a vehicle, and dumped her body where it was found. The news withheld her name, pending notification of family. I called Aline's parents, and they told me they'd just gotten word that she was the victim. I was devastated.

"The police came to talk to me that morning. I could tell they considered me a suspect. But a simple blood test proved I was innocent. They didn't even have to wait for DNA. While they were investigating, I kept in touch with the chief detective. He was kind enough to meet with me several times to let me know how the case was going, and we got to be friends. He encouraged me to consider going into law enforcement. At the age of twenty-eight, I was one of the oldest recruits at the police academy. Frankly, the strict, militaristic discipline in law enforcement isn't my style. I'd thought I was settled in my career, on my way to tenure. But after everything that happened, the change seemed right. I felt I'd be serving a greater good as a cop. Once you've been put through an experience like that—losing someone you love to a senseless, random crime—you're never the same."

"Did they ever find out who did it?"

"Actually, they did. A few months later, a student was raped by the same man. He tried to strangle her, which was how he killed

Aline. But this woman managed to escape. So they had his DNA. It matched the sample from Aline."

"Was he a student?"

"No. Just some mentally ill, homeless guy. He was living in his van near the campus. They got him on several other rapes going back a few years."

"Wow," Nicole said. "That's quite a story."

"Enough gloom and doom," he said. "The food is good here. Do you want to have dinner? Afterward, I'll follow your car to be sure you get home safe."

"What if the kidnappers are trying to get in touch with me?"

"They've had all day. They're not going to ask you to deliver the ransom tonight. You wouldn't be able to get to the bank."

"All right," she said. "Dinner, then."

At first they made awkward small talk while she tried to ignore the topic foremost on her mind. Before long they were discussing movies, books, and politics. Nicole was pleased to find that they shared many of the same views, even on law enforcement and the justice system. She was also surprised to discover Arnault could be funny. Despite her troubles, he made her laugh.

"You know, you're different than I thought when I met you," he said.

"What was your first impression?" she said. "Be honest: the brutal truth."

He took another sip of the coffee they'd ordered after their plates had been cleared away and then regarded her, as if sizing her up. "I don't know, pleasing enough to look at. You've got that deceptively sweet smile. As we talked, I could see you were cool and collected, a self-assured little package who wasn't going to take shit from anybody. And if I'm being perfectly honest, I thought you were—well—a bit of a spoiled brat with a sense of entitlement."

"Whoa," she said. "Talk about judgmental. And that impression has changed—how?"

"You are self-assured and tougher than you look," he said. "That hasn't changed. But I can also see that you're not as cool as you seemed. You have a warm side, and you're not the spoiled brat I thought you were."

"What about my sense of entitlement?"

"The jury's still out on that." He laughed. "Now you're supposed to describe your first impression of me."

"Frankly?" She took a sip of water to give herself time to think. The whole truth? That she'd found him attractive, if abrasive. That, she decided, she'd keep to herself. "I thought you had a lot of nerve coming into my office, like that, thinking you could order me around."

He shrugged. "That's par for the course. After all, that's my job. I was trying to establish a pecking order so you'd listen to me."

"But your first impression told you I wouldn't."

"And you didn't. But that was before your sister was taken, and I didn't have to worry about being sensitive. I really did think you should have stopped looking into Ashley Rexton's background. And I was right. There's some kind of connection between the Rexton kidnapping and your sister's. It's our job—I'm talking about law enforcement, not you—to figure out what that is."

"Connection? What do you mean?"

"I wish I knew," he said. "The MO makes it look like the same people who kidnapped the earlier victims also took your sister. In a city of four million people, that's a big coincidence."

Nicole glanced at her watch. It was a little after ten o'clock. "I have work tomorrow," she said. "We should go."

As they left the restaurant, he saw her to her car, which was parked a few doors down.

"I'm a couple of blocks in the other direction," he said. "Lock your car doors and wait until I pull up behind you. I'm driving a black Chevy sedan. I'll follow you home to make sure you're safe."

On the way home, she kept glancing at him in her rearview mirror. After hearing his story and spending the evening with him, she had a new perspective on Arnault. He was a nice guy, a sympathetic listener, and it had been kind of him to keep her company tonight. Then another thought occurred to her. Maybe he'd spent time with her to make sure she wasn't arranging a private deal with the kidnappers.

When they reached her block, he parked at the corner and waited until she entered her garage and drove inside. She stopped the elevator on the first floor to check her mailbox for some kind of communication from the kidnappers. There was nothing. But when she walked into her condo, she found a computer printout that had been slipped under her door. It said:

"You called the police after we warned you not to. Now the price has gone up. This is your last chance. Do not involve the police or Stephanie will die. Make no mistake. We mean business. Deliver thirty thousand dollars in $20 bills tomorrow by 11:00 p.m. at 1307 Mulholland Drive. The house is unoccupied. You'll find the gate open. Leave the money behind the potted plant on the front porch. If we are able to pick up the ransom without interference, we'll send you instructions for wiring the rest. Once we receive it, we'll release your sister."

Oh, my God, she thought. How did they know she'd called the police, when they'd been so careful to cover their tracks? Now the kidnappers were asking the impossible. How could she possibly follow their directions when the cops were following her? All she could think of was to level with Arnault and insist on going it alone. There was no other way. She got out the burner phone and called him. He didn't pick up, so she left a message. "Please call me as soon as you can," she said. "It's really important."

After she hung up, she reread the printout, noting that whoever had written it appeared to be educated. The grammar and punctuation were correct, and there were no spelling errors. She used her computer to look up the address where she was to make the drop. The property information confirmed it was indeed unoccupied and had been for over two years, tied up in a lawsuit. The owner had died without a will. Now his brother and son were fighting over who was the rightful heir. A suit had been filed in civil court, although no date was set for a hearing. Meanwhile, the house sat empty.

She switched to a map program and looked at an aerial view of the property. The house was big, as was the surrounding yard. The place had two entrances. It fronted on Mulholland, but the garage was located on the street below, providing another way into the grounds. The rear entrance would give the kidnappers a less visible route to pick up the money than the main thoroughfare in front.

Not knowing what to do with herself, she settled on the couch, put the burner phone on the coffee table, and used her cell to call the hospital. Following the phone menu, she put in David's room number so she'd be connected with him. It was late, but she thought he might be awake. Her call was diverted to the nurses' station. Nicole explained who she wanted to talk to.

"I'm afraid it's after hours for calls," The nurse said. "Why don't you try again in the morning."

"I'm his sister," Nicole lied. "Can't you at least tell me how he's doing?"

"I'm really sorry, but I can't give out patient information."

Frustrated, Nicole had to stop herself from saying something sarcastic. After all, this was hospital policy, well out of the nurse's hands. Instead, she just said, "Thanks."

She lay awake, terrified of what might happen if the police wouldn't step aside and let her deliver the money as the kidnappers demanded. She must have eventually fallen asleep because the burner phone rang at six a.m., just as it had the day before.

"You called?" Arnault said.

"I heard from them. But I can't tell you the arrangements. They knew I called the police. That's why they didn't show. This time they said they'd kill her if you're involved. So I have to deliver the ransom by myself. The advance payment has gone up to thirty thousand dollars. You were right about that. After they get the cash, they'll tell me where to wire the rest. I'm going to do what they say. I can't risk what will happen if you follow me or arrange a stakeout. I want to be clear about this. I don't care about the money. I just want my sister back."

"You're upset, and I get it. I really do. But I can't let you do this alone, Nicole. It's too dangerous. I already explained. If we're left out of the loop, both you and your sister could end up dead. Now listen carefully. This time they'll never guess we're monitoring the situation because there will be no police presence at the drop."

"How would that work?"

"We'll use a drone. After dark, it will be virtually invisible."

"I thought police weren't allowed to use drones. You know, because of—" she hesitated, figuring it might be impolitic to mention people's concerns about being spied on by the government. "Well, because of privacy issues."

"All we need is a warrant. In a case like this, no judge would refuse it."

"What if the kidnappers have night-vision binoculars?"

"You're giving these guys too much credit. It's not generally known we use drones. They won't be expecting it. I understand you picked up the money at Griffith Park. Use your lunch hour to get another thousand in twenties from the bank. I'll be at your office sometime in the afternoon to package it. Bring the kidnappers' note. Maybe we can lift prints from it."

"I doubt it. I had to open the envelope and unfold the note to see what it said. It'll have my prints on it."

"Bring it anyway, but don't touch it again. Use something to scoop it into a plastic bag. I'll pick it up when I come by."

After they hung up, she got ready for work. When she arrived at the office, she found a rush assignment on her desk. She spent the morning looking up evidence for a civil trial brought by one giant corporation against another. The work was routine and dry.

But it came as a welcome change to her search for Ashley Rexton. At noon, she went to the bank to get the money. To her relief, neither James Blagg nor Kevin James was in, and she was able to make her withdrawal without a hassle.

When she got back to work, Arnault was waiting in her office and appeared to be working on her computer.

She was more than a little annoyed. "What are you doing?"

He grinned, getting up to surrender her chair. "The woman who showed me in yesterday keeps popping by to chat. She insisted I get right to work so your computer would be ready when you got back." He raised his arms in mock helplessness. "Hey, I'm just doing my job." Once again, he was dressed like a techie, this time in jeans with a blue and green striped shirt, sleeves rolled up.

Nicole took her seat, still warm from his occupancy. From here, she could see that her computer was still on login. He hadn't been snooping; he'd been faking it. She felt herself flush.

Arnault didn't seem to notice. He closed her office door and locked it. "Can't have your buddy dropping by," he said.

Nicole was pretty sure Joanne could hear the lock click from the next office. She wondered what Joanne would think was going that would require a locked door.

Arnault started assembling the additional packets of money, sandwiching the fake bills between the real ones. When he was done, he dropped the second load of bills into the computer bag. Nicole picked it up and returned it to her cupboard. It was still surprisingly light, no more than a few pounds.

"Let me have the note they left you," Arnault said. He read it without taking it out of the plastic bag. When he was done, he tapped the address into his cell phone and studied what came up. "They were right. The house is unoccupied. It's pretty isolated; the closest neighbor is a good distance away. Go up there at least an hour early. Keep your car locked while you're driving, and minimize the time you're out of your car. Our drone has a camera, so we'll know if anything goes wrong. But it won't. We've got this. Oh, and make sure the note demanding proof of life is still in there."

By six o'clock that evening, the office had emptied out. A few minutes later, Nicole carried the computer bag down to her car and placed it on the passenger seat. She drove home, toted the bag of money up to her place, and changed from her work clothes into jeans and a sweater.

Only when she looked in the refrigerator did she realize she still hadn't had a chance to pick up groceries. Her fridge was empty except for some eggs and the bread in the freezer. She made herself a scrambled egg sandwich and carried it into the living room. After settling on the couch, she turned on the TV and ate while channel hopping. The news was too upsetting. At last, she settled on a *Seinfeld* marathon, which she barely took in, checking the clock every few minutes. Finally, at nine thirty, she decided to leave. The note had instructed her to make the drop by eleven o'clock. She figured it would take about a half hour to reach the address on Mulholland. Arnault had told her to arrive an hour early. Relieved the wait was over, she got in her car and headed through Beverly Hills and up the steep, zigzagged road through Coldwater Canyon. There was still a good deal of traffic, and she felt perfectly safe.

The house at the address she'd been given was a two-story colonial. She'd seen a photo of it on her computer's map program, but it was much bigger than she expected, perhaps six thousand square feet. The enormous yard appeared well kept and the front of the house was illuminated with several spotlights.

A six-foot wrought iron fence surrounded the property, and the gate was closed. Once parked in front, she considered how to get out of the car without attracting the notice of those driving by. She decided to exit by the passenger's door, which required an awkward climb over the transmission console. She grabbed the computer bag, closed the car door, and locked it. She hurried to the gate and pulled the latch. It swung open; she entered the front yard and closed the gate behind her. She had to make an effort not to lift her head and look for the drone. If she was being watched, that would be a tipoff that the police were monitoring the scene from overhead.

From the street, the house looked impressive and well maintained, but as Nicole got closer, she noticed signs of neglect. Several interior lights were on. Perhaps they'd been set on a timer to make the house appear occupied. What they revealed was that the windows were dirty, and there were moth holes in the drapes. Paint was peeling on the window frames; cobwebs draped corners of the front porch; and dead moths had accumulated at the bottom of the porch's light fixtures.

As Nicole climbed the half-dozen steps to the porch, she saw the potted palm behind which she'd been told to leave the money. The plant had turned brown from neglect and was drooping over the side of the pot. The place had a creepy feeling, and she sensed she was being watched. She couldn't wait to get away.

She shoved the bag of money, real and fake, behind the potted palm. Then she hurried down the stairs and all but ran to her car. She didn't bother sliding in through the passenger's door, but went around to the driver's side and locked herself in.

She went as fast as she dared down the winding road. Only when she entered her building's underground parking did she feel safe. By the time she let herself into her condo, she was exhausted but too worried and keyed up to sleep. When she was ready for bed, she set her cell and the burner phone on her night table. She lay awake wondering if the drone had succeeded in following the kidnappers to their hideout and what would happen if it hadn't.

# TWELVE

SOMETHING WOKE STEPHANIE FROM A DREAM that evaporated as soon as she opened her eyes. It was morning. She'd been coughing all night and didn't feel well enough to get out of bed. All at once, the front door slammed and footsteps clattered overhead. She could hear men's voices, loud and argumentative, although it was hard to make out what they were saying.

She forced herself to get up. Maybe her captors were here to deliver food and coffee or tea. If they did, she was going to drink whatever beverage they brought. If it put her to sleep, all the better. Anything would be an improvement over lying in bed all day, coughing and agonizing over her fate.

She grabbed her flashlight and crept up the stairs. At the top, she put her ear to the door. She could make out voices of two men. It had to be Ryan and the guy in the suit. Matt was probably laid up with his injured arm.

"No way I'm doing it," one said. His voice was high pitched and nervous.

"Well, it's not going to be me." This voice, deep and a bit

gravelly, she recognized as Ryan's. He sounded calmer and more assertive than before. "No way I'm cutting a finger off. Just the idea of touching her—"

"It won't be that bad because—" There was a loud shushing sound, and they lowered their voices. Now all she could hear was mumbling.

The hairs on Stephanie's neck stood up, and she found herself trembling. They were talking about her. They were planning to cut off one of her fingers and were fighting about which one had to do it.

The shock almost made her step backward. Just in time, she remembered the missing step. She grabbed the doorknob to catch herself. The near fall made her stomach somersault, and she felt as if she were going to be sick. She hurried down the stairs, looking for a place to hide. She went into the bathroom, but the lock was broken. Besides, the door was too flimsy to hold. One good kick would break it down.

She paused only long enough to grab the flashlight before dashing under the stairs. She shone the light around. There was nowhere to hide. All she could think of was to crouch in the shadows at the far side of the freezer. She put her back against the wall and sat down, crossing her legs in front and pulling them toward her. She listened for the basement door to open. Her heart was pounding in her ears, and she could hardly breathe.

It wasn't long before one of the men clambered down the stairs and stopped at the bottom. "Hey," he yelled. "She's not here!" Then apparently realizing his associate couldn't hear, he ran back up, shouting, "She's gone! She escaped!"

"That's impossible," the one named Ryan said. "She's got to be here. There's no way out except through that door. It was locked and nailed shut." This time both of them came down the steps.

Stephanie could see a powerful flashlight beam moving around the basement and into the crawlspace. Meanwhile, a second flashlight clicked on. The person holding it ducked under the stairs and moved the light around. It was the tall guy who'd been wearing the suit and tie, now dressed in a hoody and jeans. His light rested on her a moment before he grabbed her by the arm and pulled her to her feet. What surprised her was that he looked every bit as frightened as she felt.

"Ow," she said. "You're hurting me."

He eased his grip slightly, forcing her out of the stairwell. "I found her!" he said.

"All right," Ryan said. "Let's tie her up and get this over with."

"Right."

Sobbing, she tried to resist as they pulled her along. When Stephanie's shins hit the side of the bed, Ryan said, "Lie face down and shut your eyes. Do as I say or I'll kill you. Do you understand?"

"Ye—yes," The word came out in a stutter because her teeth were chattering. She felt her hands being tied. This struck her as odd. Why would they tie her hands together if they were planning to cut off a finger? The grip on her arms was released.

"I've got a gun," Ryan said. "Keep your head down. Don't move or I'll shoot you." She did what he said, crying into the blanket. She was shaking with fear, thinking of what they were about to do. Could someone bleed to death from a severed finger? She remembered their last visit when the guy in the suit had argued Ryan out of throwing her down the stairs or tying her up. He'd protected her that time. Was it possible he'd step in and rescue her now? Her thoughts bounced back to the conversation she'd overheard about cutting off her finger. Both men sounded as if they'd bought into the plan, although neither wanted to actually do it.

She held her breath, waiting for them to start. To her surprise, they walked away. It sounded as if they were headed for the area under the stairs. There were scuffling noises, a click, some creaking, then what sounded like the rattling of plastic. All was quiet until one yelled, "Damn it!" After that, they started muttering in a way that indicated profound frustration with whatever they were doing. They seemed to be struggling with something. After more rustling of plastic, there was a loud snap.

"See how easy that was?" Ryan said, giving an unpleasant snort of laughter. The other man didn't answer.

The door of an appliance, either the refrigerator or the freezer, was then slammed shut. When she heard footsteps approaching, she started trembling again.

One of them used a knife to cut the rope from around her wrists. He tried to grab her left hand, but she snatched it away and, out of sheer panic, rose up on her hands and knees, trying to resist.

"Stop struggling, you stupid bitch," Ryan said. "Nobody's going to hurt you. Don't just stand there," he told his partner. "Hold her down."

Someone pressed on her shoulders and put a knee in the middle of her back, forcing her to lie flat. One of them grabbed her left arm, pulling her hand out from under her. He opened her hand and stretched out her fingers. She screamed, bracing herself for what was to come.

# THIRTEEN

NICOLE GOT OUT OF BED just as the sky was beginning to show light. Her sheets and blankets were on the floor, as if she'd been struggling with them all night and the bedding had lost the battle. She was even more exhausted and depressed than when she'd gone to bed.

She was in the kitchen, making her morning coffee when she heard the burner phone ring in her bedroom. She ran to get it.

"The bastards didn't show," Arnault said.

"Oh, no!" Then, after a moment of shocked silence, she added, "Do you think they spotted the drone?"

"I don't see how. I made sure it was the same color as the sky. At the last minute, I had them paint it a lighter shade of gray because it was cloudy. Clouds reflect city lights and make the night sky brighter. By the way, I had someone on my team pick up the ransom package from the location on Mulholland. We decided it would be best if you stick to your normal routine in case the perps try to get in touch with you."

"Fine," she said. "But answer this for me. If they didn't know about the drone, and the police weren't anywhere around, how did they find out you were watching?"

"I can only guess they had another source of information. Maybe they managed to hack the burner you've been using. Have you gotten any calls that hang up right away?"

"No. The only caller I've had is you."

"Throw the phone away and get another on your way to work. Be sure to call and give me your new number. I'll have our techs give your place a sweep in case it's bugged."

"Do you need me to leave a key for the techs to come in?"

"Just your permission."

"Of course you have my permission. The note said the drop on Mulholland was our last chance to save Steph." Nicole's voice trembled, and she was on the verge of tears.

"This isn't over," he said. "These guys are desperate for money so they can get away. They'll be back with another demand."

"How can you be so sure? Maybe they'll kill Steph or abandon her and kidnap someone else. I mean, the second victim is still missing; so is Ashley. What's happened to them? Do you think they're still alive?"

"Believe me," he said. "They won't attempt another kidnapping. It's too risky. You'll be hearing from them again."

"All right." She was too upset to argue. "I'll let you know if they contact me." She hung up without waiting for his response. She was sick of his "believe me's." She was sick of him.

She opened the French doors and went out onto her small balcony as she did every morning to get an idea of the weather. It was overcast with the cloud cover left from the previous night. She gazed out at the city. Except for the occasional palm tree, the view was uninspiring. Some of the rooftops were in bad need of repair; many were cluttered with air conditioning units, satellite dishes, clotheslines, and battered lawn furniture.

Although the mail wouldn't arrive for hours, she decided to get dressed and go down to check her mailbox. If Arnault was right, another message might be waiting. The hallway was eerily silent. Less than a year old, the place still had traces of the bitter smell of new carpeting and building materials.

As she'd expected, her mailbox was empty. She took the elevator back up to her floor. Turning the corner from the elevator alcove into the second-floor hallway, she stopped. A brown cardboard box, about a foot square, was sitting in front of her door. Whoever had delivered it must have just left. The messenger couldn't have used the front door or she would have seen him. That meant he'd entered through the garage. As she thought it over, she realized that all he had to do was wait for someone to drive out and duck into the garage before the door closed. As for leaving the building, that was easy. The doors were always unlocked from inside in case of fire.

She picked up the box and shook it. It was light, and nothing rattled. She went into her place, locked the door behind her, and set the box on the kitchen table. Whoever had packed it had used copious amounts of tape, and it took a while to open. The box was packed tight with Styrofoam peanuts. She pulled them out by the handful and piled them on the table, although some rolled onto the floor.

Nested in the Styrofoam was a smaller cardboard box. She pulled off the lid to find it stuffed with crumpled newspaper. Growing more impatient, she dug into it. All at once she felt something that made her recoil and pull her hand out. It was cold and clammy, like a tiny, dead, hairless animal. It took her several minutes to gather enough courage to proceed. She drew in a deep breath, then kneeled down and dumped the box's remaining contents on the floor. Out fell what looked like a human finger. A second later, a ring tumbled out, hit the floor, and rolled into a corner.

The sight of the finger made her dizzy. Her legs gave way, and she was abruptly sitting on the floor.

She scooted back, putting some distance between herself and

the finger. It looked real enough. The thought of where it must have come from, the pain involved, made bile rise in her throat. She couldn't bring herself to take a closer look. Instead, she got up and went over to where the ring had landed. Just as she'd feared, it was Steph's engagement ring, yellow gold with a square cut ruby. She picked it up, then forced herself to go back and look at the finger. The first thing she noticed was that the fingernail was painted bright red and carefully manicured. Steph's nails were always a mess. She bit them to the quick and never bothered with a manicure.

Using some of the newspaper packing, she picked the finger up and examined it closely. The skin had an odd blue cast. She'd never seen an amputated finger before and had no way of knowing if this was normal. Bits of white bone were visible where it had been cut at the joint. There were no traces of blood.

Only now did she notice something else: this finger was too small to be her sister's. Steph, who was five-eleven, had big hands for a woman. But this finger was even smaller than Nicole's. She held the ring next to the severed finger. The ring was much too big. It would have fallen off the first time the wearer lowered her hand. The idea that the finger wasn't Steph's made it only slightly less horrifying. It had been taken from someone. But who? Were the kidnappers holding several women? Had they decided to spare Steph and chop off someone else's finger? It didn't make sense.

Something else struck her as odd. The severed finger must have been meant as a threat and should have been accompanied by a message. Where was it? She went back to the box and shook it out. Nothing. But when she dumped the remaining peanuts from the outer box, a folded sheet of paper dropped out. She caught it before it hit the floor and unfolded it:

"You made the mistake of involving the police again. We're giving you one more chance. Be warned. Next time her head will be in the box. Go about your day as usual. Bring $30,000 in a checkable bag to Union Station by 9:00 p.m. Buy a ticket out of town from Amtrak. The destination doesn't matter. You need a ticket to be able to check the bag. After you check it, go directly to the station's south patio and put the claim ticket in the planter box closest to the front wall. Come alone and, above all, do not bring the cops. Follow these instructions to the letter, or your sister dies."

She stared at the note, realizing she really had to do this on her own without letting Arnault know. But how? The police were watching her. How could she take money out of the bank without them knowing about it? How could she check a bag in a crowded train station without being observed?

With these questions dogging her, she glanced at the clock. It was 8:30 a.m. She was due at work and hadn't begun to get ready. Even if she hurried, she'd be late. She reached into the cupboard and got down the big, round Quaker oatmeal box where she hid her diamond earrings and the ring from her now defunct engagement. The box was three-quarters full of oatmeal. She put Steph's ring in a snack-sized baggy, sealed it, and buried it under the oats before returning the box to the shelf.

Next, she wrapped the finger in a paper towel, sealed it in a baggie, and put it in the refrigerator. She'd read that a severed finger could be refrigerated for several days and still be reattached. Of course, she had no more idea of when they'd cut it off than she did of whose finger it was.

She skipped breakfast, unable to think of food after handling the contents of the box. She was getting ready to leave when the phone rang.

"Hi," Arnault said. "No word yet, I assume?"

"Afraid not."

"How are you holding up?"

"Not too well." Her voice was shaky. She found herself wishing she could tell Arnault what had happened, lay her burden at his feet and have the police deal with it. But that wasn't an option.

"How about lunch?" he said. "It might help being with someone who knows what's going on."

No way, she thought. Best to spend the day avoiding him. "I have a huge amount of work waiting for me. I appreciate the offer. But talking about it isn't going change the fact that this is bad news."

"I have to admit it's worrisome," he said. "We'd expect you to have heard from them by now. But they might just be stalling to scare you into dealing with them directly. That's what they want: the cash down payment on the ransom and you in their hands to make sure you make the wire transfer. Don't fall for it."

"I won't," she said. "I promise. If I hear from them, I'll call you."

After she hung up, she thought about what came next. Once she got to work, she'd have to figure out a way to withdraw the money without being observed. If the police saw her go in the bank, Arnault would immediately hear about it and know what she was up to.

As she was on her way out the door, she had an idea. It was 8:35. The bank's staff would already be at work, even though the branch didn't officially open until ten o'clock. She went back inside, called the bank, and asked for the manager. The woman who answered the phone said he wasn't expected until late morning.

"How about Kevin James?" Nicole said. "Is he there?"

"May I say who's calling?"

"It's Nicole Graves."

Kevin was immediately on the line. "What's up, Nic—" he stopped himself and started again. "How can I provide excellent service?"

"Is that the script they make you say when you answer the phone?"

"That's right," he said. His cheerfulness sounded forced. She thought how humiliating it must be to have to say that every time the phone rang.

"Listen, Kevin. I have to make a rather large cash withdrawal, and here's the thing. I'm tied up in my office all day with back-to-back meetings. Is there any way we can arrange to have this done by messenger? I can download a withdrawal slip, fill it out, and have it delivered to you. I'll include a note authorizing you to let a messenger pick it up. You can call me when it's ready, and I'll arrange for pickup.

"How much money are we talking about?"

She hesitated only a moment before saying, "thirty thousand dollars."

"For that much cash, I'm afraid you'll have to pick it up yourself. We can't entrust that amount to a messenger. I'm really sorry, but it's bank policy."

"All right. What if I send in someone from my office with a note authorizing her to pick up the money?"

"That would work. Have this person bring a valid photo ID and a note with your signature. But make it before eleven o'clock. That's when Blagg is supposed to arrive. You're in luck that he has a dental appointment. He's taken a special interest in you and your account. If he were involved—well, it could get complicated. He'd go into his rule book and find an obscure paragraph forbidding large cash withdrawals unless the account holder picks it up in person."

"Could you pack up the money so it isn't obvious what it is? I'll have someone down there as soon as you open."

"I'm on it," Kevin said.

"Thanks so much, Kevin. I can't tell you how much I appreciate this."

"For you, Nicole," he said, "anything."

# FOURTEEN

STEPHANIE COULDN'T STOP CRYING, even after they'd let go of her, and she understood they just wanted her ring, not her finger. The two men stamped back up the stairs and slammed the door. Before long, she heard them nailing the door shut again. They drove away from the house with a loud roar of the engine. Clearly, they were angry. Was it because she'd put up a fight, or were they mad about something else? Before long, her growling stomach reminded her that she'd had nothing to eat since the previous morning. From the way her captors had left, she doubted they'd be back with food any time soon.

She lay in bed for a long time after they'd gone, listening to her heart thump. She was so hopped up on adrenaline that her illness was forgotten. Eventually, she calmed down enough to wonder about the men's behavior before they'd taken her ring. What had they been doing under the stairs?

She got up, picked up her flashlight, and went over to take a look. The spider web was gone; the guy in the suit had walked through it, and it had ended up on his clothes. She didn't hesitate before ducking under the stairs. She pulled on the refrigerator door. Except for the stale smell wafting out, it was empty. She went over to the freezer and tried to open it. A piece of heavy-duty black plastic was caught in the latch, and it was stuck shut. She tried to rip the plastic away, but it wouldn't give.

She thought of the screwdriver she'd used on the step. Retrieving it from its hiding place, she used it to pierce the plastic. She tore as much away from the latch as she could, but still it wouldn't open. Using the screwdriver as a lever, she put all her strength into forcing the latch. Suddenly the end of the screwdriver broke off. Caught off balance, she stumbled backward and landed with a thump, her tailbone hitting the cement floor. For a couple of minutes, she was immobilized with pain. When the worst had passed, she got up and went back to the freezer. The latch was now missing. The screwdriver had pried it off completely, and the lid of the freezer was open a crack. She put her fingers inside and lifted the lid.

The freezer was filled with something in a jumbo-sized black plastic trash bag. She tried lifting it, but the object inside was too heavy. The bag's opening was nowhere in sight, and she realized it must be underneath whatever this was. She jammed the business end of the broken screwdriver into the plastic and ripped a hole. When it was large enough, she picked up the flashlight and switched it on. Visible through the opening was a foot with red painted toenails. It was attached to an ankle marked with a small heart-shaped tattoo. She had no doubt the ankle was attached to a frozen, dead body. Shaking with fear and revulsion, she slammed the freezer shut, then leaned over and threw up. The flashlight slipped from her hand, hit the cement, and went out. She scrambled after it as it rolled across the floor. She had to feel around—withdrawing her hands when she encountered another spider web—until she located the flashlight. She flicked the off-and-on switch, but it no longer worked. The bulb must have broken when it hit the cement. It didn't matter. She'd seen enough.

She went back to her bed and curled up into a ball. They must have taken the finger from that body. When she'd overheard them, they hadn't been talking about her at all, but this poor, dead woman. Maybe she was one of their other victims. When Stephanie considered the implications, she felt as if she was going to be sick again.

She lay on the bed thinking about this for what seemed like hours. She was going to die here. When they checked the freezer, they'd know she'd seen the dead body. But what difference did it make? She'd already seen the faces of all three men. They were going to kill her anyway.

# FIFTEEN

As SOON AS SHE GOT TO WORK, Nicole went onto the bank's website and downloaded a withdrawal slip. She filled it out and considered how she was going to ask Joanne to carry out this secret mission. She and Joanne were friendly, even though they rarely socialized outside of work. Nicole was sure that Joanne was honest and could be trusted with a secret.

She quickly dashed off a note authorizing Joanne Bates to pick up the money, put the note and withdrawal slip in an envelope, and wrote Kevin's name on it. Then she went into Joanne's office and closed the door. "I need to ask a favor, and I'd be eternally grateful if you'd do it without asking questions. I'll explain everything when I can, which might not be for a day or two."

"Now you've really piqued my curiosity," Joanne said. "What do you need me to do?"

"Just take this envelope to the bank downstairs and give it to the assistant manager, Kevin James. He's expecting it. He'll give you a package, and you'll bring it to me."

"Of course," Joanne said. "And I'll keep my questions to

myself." She gestured zipping her lips.

Ten minutes later, Joanne was back with a box about the same size as the one that had been left at Nicole's door that morning.

"Thanks so much, Joanne. I really owe you. As soon as I can, I'll explain. I promise."

Nicole took the box, went into her office and closed the door. She'd just finished locking the money in the cupboard where she kept her purse and jacket when she thought of something. Why had the kidnappers failed to show up at the first two drops? After the first drop failed, Arnault asked her if she'd told anyone. She hadn't, and the police took extra care on the second drop, when they'd used the drone to keep watch. Somehow the kidnappers still found out the cops were involved.

Suddenly it dawned on her. The bank had records of her withdrawals. If the kidnappers had access to that information, they'd see she'd taken out only two thousand dollars, not the twenty thousand dollars they'd asked for. It wouldn't take a genius to figure out that someone, most likely the police, was setting a trap. Had the kidnappers hacked into the bank's computer system? It had been done at other financial institutions. She thought of her conversation with Kevin that morning, his nonplussed attitude when she asked for thirty thousand dollars. How often did people withdraw that much in cash? Wouldn't he have expressed a little curiosity or sounded surprised? She remembered his tone of voice when he'd said, "For you Nicole, anything." It was as if he'd been expecting her call.

She sat down at her desk and was about to type in Kevin's name for a background check when there was a knock at her door. She called, "Come in."

To her surprise, it was Arnault, carrying a cardboard tray with two cups of coffee and a white paper bag with the logo of the pastry shop across the street. He gave her a big smile. "You couldn't do lunch, but I knew you'd have to take a morning break. At least ten minutes; it's the law."

"How kind of you to come and personally enforce it." She gave him a smile, feeling relieved on two counts. She'd already gotten the cash to pay the kidnappers. She'd also been lucky that Arnault hadn't arrived a few minutes earlier. If he had, he'd have come up in the elevator with Joanne and seen her hand the box to Nicole. How could that have not aroused his curiousity?

"So, what did you bring me?" she said.

He unfolded the top of the bag and held it out to her. She reached in and pulled out a jelly donut. It looked delicious. She took a bite, and it was. "Yum," she said. "Thanks."

They talked companionably for a short time, which turned out to be ten minutes, when Nicole glanced at her watch. He must have noticed because he stood and said, "Party's over. Back to work. Give me a call if—"

"You know I will," she said.

She stayed in at lunch, picking up a turkey sandwich from Charlotte, the woman who called each morning with her basket of luncheon fare, fruit, and cookies. Nicole realized she wouldn't be able to stop at the grocery store after work, not with all that cash in the car. Instead, she bought a salad and some banana bread to bring home for dinner. Nicole got her purse out to pay, careful to relock the cupboard. After Charlotte left, Nicole dug into work again, leaving her purse sitting on her desk.

Despite everything that was going on, Nicole was able to focus on work for the first time since Stephanie disappeared. She wondered if it was because she'd regained control of the situation and was no longer under the thumb of the police. Around three o'clock, she was startled by a knock on her door. It was Arnault again, this time carrying two tall cups from Ringo's coffee house.

"No word yet," she said, before he had a chance to ask.

"We've had a tip about an abandoned house in Laurel Canyon that's suddenly seeing a lot of activity," he said. "We sent a team up there to take a look."

"You don't sound very hopeful."

"People call in tips that usually come to nothing, but we've got to check them out. I have to confess I'm worried you haven't heard anything by now."

"I know," Nicole said quietly. She had to play dumb, but she wasn't sure she was giving a convincing performance. She grabbed a tissue from the box on the shelf behind her and dabbed at her eyes.

"Dinner tonight?" he said.

She hesitated, trying to think of an excuse. "I'm afraid I won't be very good company."

"That's why I'm asking. I know how hard it will be for you to wait by yourself."

"All right," she said. "I haven't been sleeping, so I'm hoping to grab a nap when I get home. Why don't you come around nine o'clock, and we'll go out for something to eat." Even as she said this, she knew that by the time he arrived to pick her up, she'd have left to deliver the ransom.

He set the coffee drinks on her desk, pushed one over to her, and sat down.

She took a sip of hers. "This is yummy. What is it?"

"Caramel macchiato," he said. "My favorite."

"Thanks for bringing it. That was really thoughtful."

He smiled. "You're very welcome."

They lapsed into an awkward silence. After a few moments, Arnault picked up the ball, filling her in on the latest news— an exposé about the city's continuing failure on the issue of homelessness. When Nicole glanced at her watch, Arnault stood up. "I guess it's time for me to go," he said.

As she walked him to the door, he said, "Keep your spirits up. This game ain't over yet." They looked into each other's eyes for a long moment before he turned and, after a brief goodbye, left.

She closed the door after him and leaned against it, thinking how mad he'd be when he learned she'd skipped out on him, that she was doing exactly what he'd warned her not to, dealing directly with the kidnappers. The money might well allow them to sneak out of the country. Arnault's case would be blown, and it would be her doing. But what did it matter. She'd probably never see him again. In a way, she was sorry. But she felt sure that, even if she'd met him under different circumstances, it wouldn't have worked out.

When quitting time arrived, she was calm and focused on what was about to happen. She took the box out of the cupboard and set the food she'd bought on top. She carried the load down to the garage to put in the trunk of her car. After arriving at her condo building, she carted everything to the second floor.

Stepping off the elevator, she glanced out the big window that offered a view of the street. The glass was tinted so no one could see in. A gray sedan had just pulled up to the curb across the street. Instead of getting out, the driver rolled down the window. She watched while he lit a cigarette and settled back in his seat. He'd parked so he had a view of her building's front door as well as the entrance to the garage. She had no doubt he was a cop and that Arnault had sent him to keep an eye on her. It was just what she'd expected. Her next challenge would be to leave the building without being seen. She'd figured out a plan but had yet to make the arrangements.

She carried her things into her place. Her calm had somehow evaporated, along with any appetite she might have had. She stuck the salad and banana bread in the refrigerator and went into the living room to turn on the news. All at once she remembered something she'd intended to do that afternoon, before Arnault arrived and distracted her.

She went into her office, turned on the computer and typed Kevin's name, first into her search engine, then her office database. He'd had a DUI when he was a 19, a serious offense since he wasn't old enough to drink. He'd had his license taken away for a year and was sentenced to community service. Other than that, his record was clean. But under financial information, the picture wasn't exactly rosy. His credit rating was borderline at 400. If it were much lower, he would have been considered a bad credit risk. The worst news was that, four years out of college, he owed two hundred twenty thousand in student loans. He'd only begun to pay them back the previous year, when he'd started as a management trainee with the bank. Even with these financial problems, it was hard for Nicole to believe that meek-mannered Kevin James would get involved in a crime as serious as kidnapping.

She took a look at his social media page. He was given to posting cartoons and snapshots of meals he'd had at restaurants. Some photos showed him with people who, for the most part, weren't identified. But two were consistently tagged with their names: Ryan Holich and Matthew Bissell. In one shot, they were wearing suits and ties. It looked like some kind of graduation event. A banner behind them said "Congratulations Olympia Bank Management Trainees."

Nicole's scalp tingled with the thrill of discovery. They all worked for the same bank. She'd never seen Kevin's buddies before, so she figured they worked in other branches. The threesome were also shown in the same apartment. Either they hung out a lot at one guy's place, or they were roommates.

She switched to Ryan's Facebook page. It showed some of the same photos that were on Kevin's. His posts talked about his work. She was surprised to learn that Ryan, like Kevin, was a management trainee with Olympia bank, but at a different branch. Looking farther, she saw that Ryan's credit rating was no better than Kevin's.

Matthew was also with the same bank at yet another branch. He held a similarly low credit rating. All three were burdened with student debt. Of more interest were two photos Matthew had posted of himself with a woman. In one they had their arms around each other. In the other they were cheek to cheek. The woman had short, wildly curly, dark hair and big, round, black-rimmed glasses. It was Ashley Rexton in disguise. The dark hair, curls, and glasses had completely changed her look. Nicole hovered her cursor over the photo to see if her name appeared, but she wasn't tagged. What had she been thinking, allowing someone to take her photo? Obviously, she had no idea Matthew would be dumb enough to post it on social media.

Nicole thought about the bank connection. The three men— Kevin, Ryan, and Matthew—all worked for Olympia Bank. It would have been easy for them to find out about her withdrawals. How had they chosen the other victims? Was it through their bank accounts? The name of the first victim had never been made public. Nicole looked up the second victim, Victoria Reina, and found she and her husband shared a wealth management account with Olympia Bank. And finally, Nicole checked Ashley herself. She also banked with Olympia. There it was, she thought, the link between all three kidnappings that Arnault had talked about.

Just then, Nicole heard the neighbor she'd been waiting for arrive home. She got up and went over to knock on the door. Michelle was a legal secretary, pale and prim with fair hair worn in a chignon. She'd seemed unfriendly when Nicole first moved in, but later Nicole realized the woman was extremely shy. One evening, Michelle showed up at Nicole's door in her bathrobe and explained, between bouts of coughing, that she had the flu. She'd timidly asked if Nicole would mind picking up her prescription. She'd had her doctor phone it in to a drugstore a few blocks away, only to discover that it didn't deliver. She was too sick to go herself.

Nicole had not only gotten the prescription, but she'd picked up groceries for Michelle until she recovered, about a week later. That had sealed their friendship. Michelle was now in the habit of dropping by to talk to Nicole, whom she seemed to regard as some kind of guru on relationships. Michelle had none. At the age of twenty-nine, she was eager to find someone but was too shy to sign up for Internet dating.

When Michelle's door opened, Nicole said, "I wonder if I could ask you a favor."

"Of course, of course," Michelle said, waving her in. "How about a glass of wine? It's that time of day."

"Sure," Nicole said. "I could use it."

When they each were seated with their drinks, Michelle said, "You needed a favor. Tell me what I can do."

"I'm being stalked," Nicole said.

Michelle's eyes widened and her mouth rounded into an 'O' before she said. "Stalked? By who?"

"This guy I met through the Internet. I said 'no' to a second date, but he wouldn't listen. When I ghosted his messages, he started stalking me." Nicole was making this up as she went along. "Tonight he followed me home from work." She got up and beckoned Michelle to follow her down the hall to the elevator alcove. They stopped at the big window. The cop was still sitting in his car across the street.

"That's him in the gray car," Nicole said.

"Have you called the police?"

"Every time I call them, he just ducks out of sight until they leave. It's hopeless. If this keeps up, I'll have to move."

"Oh, Nicole, don't do that. What can I do to help?"

Observing Michelle's distress, Nicole wondered if she'd overdone it. She'd worked hard to encourage Michelle to sign up for online dating. This might make her think she'd end up with a stalker, too.

"I need a ride, that's all," Nicole said. "I'll move in with my sister until this guy gives up. But he knows my car, so I'll have to get to Steph's another way. I'm wondering if you'd drive me to the Metro Station at Wilshire and La Brea. I'll duck down so he won't be able to see me leave in your car."

"You don't have to take Metro," Michelle said. "I'll be happy to drive you to your sister's."

"That's not necessary," Nicole said quickly. "Traffic is terrible at this hour. The subway will be quicker. I just need a few minutes to change and pack an overnight bag."

"Come back whenever you're ready."

Nicole went back to her place, put the money in her overnight bag, and changed into jeans, an old t-shirt, and, since the nights were still cool, a warm jacket. She took her cell and the burner phone out of her purse and set them on her bureau. She could be tracked, she knew, by her cell. She wasn't sure about the burner phone. But since she'd used it to communicate with Arnault, there was the possibility he could use it to locate her whereabouts. No sense taking chances. Looking in the mirror, she pulled her hair into a ponytail and covered it with a faded blue baseball cap with the word "chill" on it. It had belonged to Josh, her ex-fiancé. Somehow, she hadn't been able to part with it.

Michelle seemed genuinely spooked as she accompanied Nicole to the elevator and down to the garage. She kept looking around, as if she expected to be accosted by the stalker. As they drove out of the garage, Nicole bent down so she couldn't be seen. After several blocks she sat up and looked out the back window. There was plenty of traffic but no sign of the gray car.

Nicole had to wait just a few minutes before a train arrived. She boarded, and it silently headed east toward downtown. It was rush hour on a Friday, and every seat was taken. She had to hang onto a pole with her free arm wrapped tightly around her overnight bag. After a short time, however, a young man got up and offered her his seat. From his clothes, soiled from construction or yard work, she could see he was a working-class Latino like many others on the train. He looked beat. Ordinarily, she would have refused the seat, but her bag was getting heavy, and if someone grabbed it, she'd be unable to hold onto it with only one hand.

It was a relief to sit down with a firm grip on the bag of money. After another fifteen minutes, the train arrived at Union Station. Some years before, it had been restored to its original art deco glory. The refurbished complex included several upscale restaurants, as well as a garden and big rooms for weddings and other events.

Clasping the bag against herself, she passed countless men and women making their way to and from the trains. When she reached the Amtrak ticket office, there was a long line, snaking back and forth in a Z, along a rope divider. With a sigh, she fell into step at the end. Looking around at the people crowding the station, she did a double take at the sight of perhaps thirty Amish in their old-fashioned outfits with bonnets and hats. They ranged from babes in arms to old timers with long white beards, making their way from the trains to the street. She wondered what would have impelled them to travel by train, since they usually went to great lengths to avoid modern conveyances.

At last it was her turn at the window. She bought the cheapest train ticket on offer, a one-way to San Diego. She checked the bag with the ticket agent, who passed it to a baggage handler. He put the bag on a trolley brimming with luggage.

She turned and, following the note's instructions, hurried through the door that bore a sign reading, "South Patio." Walking in the direction of the entrance, she stopped at the front-most planter box, which held a blooming crepe myrtle. Its magenta blossoms were just beginning to fade. She was about to put the claim ticket in the tree's planter box when she spotted a manila envelope sitting on top of the soil. In big block letters, it said, "Nicole." She picked it up.

There was a paragraph printed beneath her name. It said, "Go back and reclaim your bag immediately. This was a test to make sure you didn't bring the cops. You are being watched. Hurry before they put the bag on the train."

Nicole arrived in the lobby just as the baggage handler was wheeling his trolley into a long corridor that led to the train platforms. She ran after him, shouting "Wait, wait!" But the din of the station drowned out her voice. She was almost upon him before he heard her and turned around. She held out her claim stub, almost too breathless to speak. "I've changed my mind," she gasped. "I'm not taking the train after all."

The man was young, slightly built, and not much taller than Nicole. He didn't look strong enough to be in the business of lifting heavy bags. Hearing her request, his face colored and registered an expression of extreme annoyance. He grabbed her ticket and began digging through the pile of bags on his cart, tossing some on the floor as he searched for hers. When he found it, he thrust it into her arms.

"Next time, think before you pull a stunt like this. Now these bags will probably miss the train. I hope you're happy." He scrambled to stack the tossed bags back on the trolley and took off at a run.

The envelope she'd retrieved from the planter was crumpled in her hand. She went over to a bench, placed her bag on her lap, and smoothed out the envelope. Her stomach was knotted with anxiety. As she read the kidnapper's instructions, it struck her that whoever was choreographing this ransom drop had no idea what he was doing.

# Sixteen

It wasn't until evening that the flap in the door opened and something slid onto the shelf. Stephanie hadn't heard the car arrive. Until today, sounds from the top of the stairs had sent her rushing up to see if her captors had brought something to eat. Now, feeling ill and overwhelmed by a sense of doom, she couldn't summon the energy to get up from the bed.

A few minutes passed before the flap opened again. "Hey, Stephanie!" a man called out, "Come up here. I've brought you some food." She recognized the voice. It was the guy in the suit.

"I'm not hungry," she yelled.

"Please come up," he said. "I want to talk to you. I'm alone this time. I know how scared you must be, and I have good news. I also brought a really nice meal for a change. Come see."

Slowly, Stephanie got up and climbed the stairs. The flap in the door was open, and she could see the man on the other side of the door. He actually looked cheerful, as if he really was the bearer of good news. "Your sister's finally delivering the ransom," he said. "This time tomorrow, you'll be home."

Her temper flared. "I don't believe you. You're not even in charge, are you? Somebody else makes all the decisions."

"I'd never let anyone hurt you," he said. "The guy who was with me last time wanted to throw you down the stairs, and I stopped him. Remember?"

"What about the woman in the freezer? Did you tell her she was going home?"

He was silent and looked away, as if he couldn't face her accusation. Finally, he said. "That was an accident. One of the top steps broke, and she fell straight through to the basement floor. We weren't even here when that happened."

"Right." Stephanie didn't bother to hide her skepticism.

"It's the truth. You don't have to believe me, but we really are letting you go. I just want you to promise me one thing."

"Like, what?"

"That you won't identify me to the police."

"How could I? I don't even know your name."

"Well, what if the police catch us? I don't think they will but suppose they do, and you see me in a lineup. Promise you'll say you've never seen me before."

"I promise." She did her best to sound sincere. Of course, she'd identify him in a lineup. How could he be naive enough to imagine she wouldn't? "Are you really alone here?"

"Yes."

"I believe you really do care what happens to me. Since no one else is around, why not let me go? I'm afraid of that guy who was with you this morning. If he has his way, I'll end up with the woman in the freezer. I'll keep out of sight until you collect the ransom. You have my word. You can tell your friends that when you got here, the door to the basement was open, and you have no idea how I got out. And I'll tell the police you were all wearing masks, and I can't identify anyone."

"I can't let you go just yet, Stephanie." His tone was patient, as if he was explaining the situation to a small child. "We have to keep you here until we get the money. Try to understand. We're in a lot of trouble. We have to get out of the country before the police track us down." He paused and looked at his watch. "Oh, my God. I've got to go. Check out what's on the tray. It's from the food bar at Bristol Farms. I even brought a bottle of wine and dessert."

"Before you leave, can you at least give me another flashlight?" she said. "The other one stopped working."

The flap dropped shut, and she heard him walk away. Almost immediately, he was back, handing her a small flashlight. "Just remember what I said about keeping quiet." With that, he closed the flap and locked it.

She used the flashlight to take a look at what he'd brought. A white bag contained a Styrofoam food container, plastic cutlery, and a screw-top bottle of wine. Next to the bag stood a super-sized cup of soda.

It took her three trips to carry the food and drinks downstairs. The whole time she kept wondering if the woman really had died by accident. It was true that Matt had been lucky he'd rolled downstairs instead of falling through the hole made by the displaced step. It was at least a twelve-foot drop to the concrete floor.

Maybe the man had been telling the truth. That step had been replaced recently. And it was possible that a weakened step could have given way when the woman put her weight on it. Stephanie wished she could believe this story instead of the one stuck in her head, that these men had murdered the woman because she'd have been able to identify them.

She set the food container on the bed, lifted the lid, and turned on the flashlight. The container held a generous portion of roast beef, potatoes and gravy, along with what looked like spinach soufflé. At the edge of the plate, now partially covered with gravy, was a slice of cherry cheesecake. The smell of food made her feel sick. She sipped a little of the soda. It turned out to be cherry cola, which had always reminded her of cough syrup. She unscrewed the cap of the wine bottle and took a swig. Yes, she thought, this would do the trick.

She closed the Styrofoam container and took it up to the shelf at the top of the stairs so she wouldn't have to smell the food. For the first time within memory, Stephanie wasn't hungry.

# SEVENTEEN

THE NOTE NICOLE HAD FOUND in the planter box at Union Station contained instructions for delivering the ransom to an address on Kirkwood Drive. She was to leave the bag of money behind a couch on the porch.

"The house is set back from the street," the note said. "There is no porch light, so bring a flashlight. Do not make the mistake of getting the police involved this time. Come alone or you'll never see your sister again."

She had no idea where Kirkwood Drive was. Since she'd left her cell phone behind, she couldn't look it up. Instead, she went to the station's visitors' information booth, where a white-haired woman was sitting behind the counter. She had a kind face and looked delighted as Nicole approached. It made Nicole wonder how many travelers used this service when people could easily look up directions, train schedules, and even a map of the station's interior on their cell phones. The woman's nametag identified her as DeeDee, although it was hard to imagine anyone looking less like a DeeDee. Nicole showed her the Kirkwood address and asked for directions.

"9780 Kirkwood Drive," DeeDee repeated. She lifted a pair of white-framed glasses hanging from a chain around her neck and put them on. After tapping the address into her computer, she narrowed her eyes and leaned forward to read the map on her screen. "Kirkwood is north of Sunset, just off Laurel Canyon Boulevard. There's no public transportation up there at this hour. You'll have to drive, take a taxi, or call Uber." Just then, the printer next to her lit up and a page emerged. DeeDee glanced at it, then handed it to Nicole. It was a map with driving directions from the station to the Kirkwood address.

After thanking DeeDee, Nicole left the information booth and sat on a nearby bench to study the map. The prospect of having to go to yet another location in order to pay the ransom made her feel defeated and exhausted. She had to arrive alone, but she didn't have her car. Nor did she have a flashlight, only a tiny gadget on her keychain with a beam just bright enough to guide a key into a lock. One step at a time, she told herself. First, the car—there had to be a car rental agency somewhere near the station. She went back to DeeDee at the information booth.

"Can I rent a car around here?"

"Yes, dear, there's a Budget rental agency not too far away." The woman pointed toward the exit. "Go outside, turn left and then left again. Walk all the way to the street at the rear of the station and turn right. Keep going for another—" she paused, apparently figuring out the distance, before adding, "five or six blocks. Actually, it's a bit of a hike. Why don't you give them a call? They'll pick you up in front of the station."

"I forgot my phone. Can you direct me to the pay phones?"

"I'm afraid they took them out." The woman shook her head, as if the idea of it mystified her as much as it did Nicole. "It was about the same time they got rid of the storage lockers."

Great, Nicole thought. When it came to what people need when they use public transportation, the transit district still didn't get it. She thanked the woman and headed for the exit, planning to walk over to the rental agency, however long that took. Out the front door and halfway down the stairs, she stopped, struck by a thought. Arnault would know by now that she'd stood him up, and he'd probably have figured out what she was up to. If she rented a car, she'd have to use a credit card. Law enforcement had access to credit card activity. But did rental car agencies track the whereabouts of each of their vehicles in real time? Did they hand such information over to the police? She had no idea, but she didn't want to risk it.

Without a phone, she couldn't even summon Uber. There were plenty of taxis in front of the station, but that wouldn't work either. Taking a cab to the address meant she wouldn't arrive alone, which was what the kidnappers demanded. She walked the rest of the way down the steps and paused in front of the station, trying to figure out what to do. At that moment, a shiny black sedan with an Uber sticker in the window pulled up to drop off several passengers. She unzipped her gym bag and tugged some twenties from one of the bundled packs. After rezipping the bag, she hurried over to the car and reached it just as the last passenger was getting out. Before he had a chance to close the door, Nicole climbed in.

"Hey," the driver said. "You have to get out. The only way to get a ride with Uber is to request it through our app. I'm not allowed to pick up random passengers. Besides, somebody's waiting for me over there." He gestured toward some people standing by the steps.

"Hold on," she said. "I'm about to make you an offer you can't refuse."

"I told you. I'm not allowed—"

He stopped talking when Nicole held up the twenties and flipped through them, counting to herself. "I've got $220 here. It's yours if you'll sign out of Uber and take me where I want to go: Kirkwood Drive off Laurel Canyon Boulevard. You know where that is?"

"No. And if I sign out, I can't use my GPS, or Uber will know I've broken the rule against picking you up like this."

"No problem. I have directions." She waved the map at him and turned on the dome light to check it. "Get on the Hollywood Freeway heading north, and I'll tell you where to get off."

Just then, the door next to Nicole opened, and a woman was standing there with two suitcases. She gave Nicole a withering look. "This is my ride," she said. "Get out."

"I'm sorry but you're mistaken," the driver said. "This lady is my passenger. If your driver didn't show, you'll have to request another one."

"See this?" she said, holding out her phone. "Your license number is right here, and your name is Daniel. Isn't that right? I've been standing here for twenty minutes, waiting for you."

The driver got out of the car, and Nicole got a better view of him. He was a Latino in his early twenties, tall, broad-shouldered, and good-looking.

He approached the woman and spoke politely but quite firmly. "I'm very sorry, but the app must have double booked me. I picked up this passenger first. So, I'm afraid you'll have to contact Uber and ask for another driver." He closed the door she'd left open and returned to the driver's seat. As soon as the woman was back on the sidewalk, he drove away.

As Nicole considered what her next move would be, she decided it might be useful to establish rapport with Daniel. Most Uber drivers seemed to like talking to passengers, and many considered the job a stopgap until they made it in their chosen field. They were artists, musicians, actors, or simply between jobs.

"So, let me guess, Daniel," Nicole said. "You're an actor when you're not driving for Uber. Right?"

He laughed. "Wrong. I'm a student at Loyola."

"Wow," she said. "That's impressive. What are you studying?"

"I'm taking their core curriculum. Basically, it's pre-law."

"You're headed for law school?"

"That's the plan."

"What made you want to become a lawyer?" Nicole only half-listened while he explained. Her mind was racing ahead. She couldn't have this man drive her to the house on Kirkwood. She had to arrive alone. But how? Slowly a plan hatched. She'd have to dip into the ransom money again, this time for a larger amount. One thousand dollars? Two? How much would it take? She quietly unzipped the bag of money and withdrew a banded packet containing two thousand dollars in twenties. Daniel couldn't turn this down, could he?

It was almost nine p.m., and Laurel Canyon above Sunset was quiet. Most of the houses were dark and looked as if no one was home. The neighborhood, built along a twisty uphill portion of the road, represented an eclectic mix of expensive, recently built homes and older houses, some of them neglected and tumbledown. The latter were probably rentals or inhabited by old-time residents. Nicole wondered if most people who lived here were out for the evening or if the more upscale houses were second homes to people who preferred to spend this time of year elsewhere.

At the corner of Laurel Canyon and Kirkwood, she told Daniel to stop. "How much would you charge to let me use your car tonight?" she said. "I'll get it back it to you in the morning."

He turned around and gaped at her. "Are you out of your mind? I owe a fortune on this car. No way I'm lending it to a stranger." He paused a moment, considering his words, then added, "No offense. But I don't even know who you are."

"How much?" she repeated, switching on the dome light and holding up the bundle of bills. It was held together by a lavender paper band marked "$2,000."

Daniel opened his mouth to object, closed it, and swallowed hard. His eyes kept darting back and forth between Nicole and the packet of cash. He really wanted the money. At the same time, he was afraid he'd never see his car again. "How can I be sure you'll return it?" he said.

"I'll leave you my American Express gold card."

"How do I know it's not maxed out?"

"I guess you'll have to trust me."

He thought about it for a while. "You have more than one credit card?"

"I've got three, counting my debit card."

"Okay. Give me your wallet. That way I'll have your driver's license. The credit cards will be your collateral."

"I'll be needing my driver's license. You can have my wallet. Use your phone to take a photo of my license so you'll have my name and address."

"It's a deal," he said.

She took out her drivers' license. He snapped a photo, and she handed over the packet of bills, along with her wallet. He jotted his phone number and address down on a piece of paper and handed it to her. "You'll call me first thing tomorrow to arrange the car's return, right?"

"Right," she said. "First thing."

After he got out of the car, Nicole slid into the drivers' seat, pulling it forward so her feet reached the pedals.

"Wait a minute," he said. "How am I supposed to get home?"

"Send for an Uber, Daniel. You can afford it."

She turned the key in the ignition and started up Kirkwood. She glanced at the addresses painted on the curb. The house she wanted was at least ten blocks farther on. The street grew narrower as she drove. Finally, she reached the 2900 block and what she thought might be the right place. But no address was painted on the curb, and the lot was so overgrown with trees and shrubs that she couldn't see the house. She pulled forward and then backed up to check the addresses on either side—both some distance away. This had to be it.

She parked in front and used the light on her keychain to

navigate through the trees and shrubs at the front of the property. As she shoved her way through, thorny branches grabbed at her jeans and the sleeves of her jacket. Twice, she stumbled over fallen branches and jumped back when a small creature scurried across her path. About sixty feet in, she emerged from under the trees. The moon was a pale, skinny crescent, providing just enough light for her to see a small wooden house built into the hill. The structure appeared deserted. Its dilapidated state dated it back to the days when this area was the domain of hippies and recluses.

In the silent darkness, the place looked creepy, as if something menacing were waiting inside. The house had a steep stairway that reached to what looked like the second floor with a landing halfway up. She climbed up to the landing where she found the couch mentioned in the kidnappers' note. It was made of wicker, weather-beaten and on the verge of collapse. A cat was curled up on it, fast asleep. When the porch creaked under Nicole's feet, the animal woke, hunched its back, and hissed at her before jumping off the couch and scuttling down the stairs. Nicole had to move the couch away from the wall to wedge the bag behind it. Once this was done, she rushed back to the darkness of the yard.

She stood there a long moment, staring at the house. It was hard to resist the urge to find a way inside and see if Steph was here. But it was possible the kidnappers had chosen this spot for a ransom drop because it was vacant and isolated, like the house on Mulholland. In any case, she couldn't go in now. The kidnappers might be here any time to pick up the money. She couldn't risk having them find her there.

She was heading back to where she'd parked when she had an idea. She could hide in the car and wait for them to come for the money. If they left without going into the house, it probably meant Steph wasn't here. In that case, she'd follow them, hoping they'd lead her to their hiding place. If that didn't pan out, she'd could always come back and check out this house.

Only when she got back to the car did she realize she couldn't leave it parked where it was. The street was too narrow for another vehicle to pass, and signs forbidding parking were posted on both sides. She'd have to park somewhere else. The question was where. She drove up the hill past the next house, which also was dark and deserted-looking. Next to it was what appeared to be a vacant lot.

It was overgrown with vines that—in the black of night—looked like kudzu but were probably ivy or morning glory. She slowly eased the car deep into the foliage, hoping she didn't bump into anything that would scratch Daniel's shiny black car.

She got out and, after making sure the car couldn't be seen from the road, walked down to the house where she'd left the money. She struggled her way through the foliage again and scoped out the yard for the best place to hide. On one side of the property was a giant fir tree with branches that almost touched the ground. She burrowed under the lowest branches. It made the perfect hiding place. She couldn't be seen, but gaps between dried needles on the lower branches provided a view of the yard. She was alert to every creak and crackle, every rustle of the tall, dry weeds. Coyotes roamed these canyons along with possums, raccoons, owls, hawks and other nocturnal birds, as well as the occasional mountain lion. People living in places like this had to make sure their pets were in at night.

An hour passed, then another, but no one came. She was half dozing when headlights coming up the hill alerted her. A car pulled up, parked in front, and a man got out. It was too dark for her to see who it was. He turned on a powerful flashlight and followed a path she hadn't seen leading to the house. She watched as he climbed the stairs to the landing, reached behind the couch, and retrieved the bag. Without hesitation, he hurried back to his car. The dome light went on. No doubt he was checking to be sure there was cash in the bag and that it was the real thing.

When he started up his engine, Nicole crawled out from under the branches and ran for her car. Meanwhile, it took the man several tries to complete a U-turn on the narrow street. He was just starting down the hill when she reached her car. She didn't dare turn on her headlights. But even without them, she managed to back out of the vine-covered lot without mishap.

As she started downhill, she could see the glint of taillights several blocks ahead. She was focused on maneuvering the dark, curving street. At the same time, she was aware how dangerous it was to be doing this on her own. No one knew where she was. She almost regretted not telling Arnault. But he couldn't be trusted to keep it between the two of them. At this point, with the kidnapper in sight, he'd call for backup, summoning a fleet of squad cars.

She was able to see the car until it reached the intersection where Kirkwood ended and he had to turn onto Laurel Canyon. When she reached the intersection, she paused to look in both directions. Downhill, she could see the glow of taillights. A car was waiting at a traffic signal on Sunset. Praying this was the right car, she pressed her foot to the accelerator and sped down the canyon road. She slowed as she approached the other car and stopped a distance behind it.

She couldn't believe her luck. It was the same car she'd seen at the house. Keeping her distance, she followed it down the hill into the area of Hollywood below Melrose. It turned onto a narrow side street and pulled up in front of a double row of small 1920s-era bungalows. Most of these courtyard apartments, once ubiquitous here, had been replaced by big apartment buildings as the neighborhood gentrified. The man got out of the car. Under the streetlight, it was easy for her to identify him as Ryan. With the bag of ransom money on his shoulder, he climbed the three steps at the front of the yard and went into one of the units. The bungalows were tiny with no more than two small bedrooms, if that. Nicole didn't think it would be possible to hold anyone prisoner here. One shout would alert the neighbors.

Her thoughts went back to the house on Kirkwood. Steph

was probably there. The place had all the requisites: neighbors a good distance away, house hidden from the street. The way it was built into the hillside meant there might be a basement to hold the furnace and water heater. Most houses in L.A. didn't have basements. But the way this one was constructed offered the perfect place to hide a prisoner.

She waited, resisting the urge to speed back to Kirkwood Drive. She had a hunch that the others involved in the kidnapping would show up to collect their cut of the money. Nicole rummaged around in her purse for pen and paper to write down the address of the courtyard apartment. Aside from her pen, all she could find was an old grocery receipt. It would have to do.

After looking around to be sure no one was watching, she got out of the car. There was no street number on the bungalows, but the number was painted on the curb—201. She walked up the three steps in front and noted that the bungalow the man had entered was No. 5. She went back to the sidewalk and walked to the corner, where she found a street sign that said "Acacia Way." After writing down the address, she carefully folded the receipt and put it in the pocket of her jacket. Then she hurried back to her car to wait.

About a half hour passed before a car with another man arrived and parked nearby. As he got out, she could see it was Kevin. He went into the same bungalow Ryan had entered. Minutes later, a woman showed up in a flashy sports car and got out. It was impossible to tell if it was Ashley. She was wearing a loose-fitting jacket with the hood up and baggy pants. She opened the trunk of her car and retrieved two large grocery bags. Then she, too, disappeared into the same bungalow.

Nicole waited another five minutes to see if any of them made a move to leave, but nothing happened. Maybe the woman, whoever she was, had brought food and drink, and they were going to spend the night celebrating their good fortune. At least, that's what Nicole hoped.

She went around the block and headed back to Kirkwood Drive. When she reached the house, she hid the car in same place as before.

Once more, she got out her mini flashlight and turned it on. The beam was getting dimmer, so she turned it off to save the battery. The moon had disappeared behind a cloud, and it was even darker than before. She used her hand to guide herself along the cyclone fence that ran up the property line alongside the house. At one point, she thought she heard footsteps in the dry grass behind her. She stopped and turned to look. Everything was quiet, but it was so dark that it was impossible to see. She took a few more steps, then she stopped again to listen. Nothing. Maybe the sounds she'd heard were made by an animal.

As she neared the house, the crescent moon came out again, and she stopped to gaze up. There were no windows on the enclosed space below the first landing. She wasn't sure if this was the first floor, a basement, or simply crawl space that had been walled in to keep out the critters inhabiting the canyon. But there was a window in the door at the very top of the stairs, making it look like the main entrance to the house. It was quite a climb.

She'd have to figure out how she was going to get in. She had a Swiss Army knife on her keychain. It included a metal toothpick that supposedly doubled as a lock pick. She'd never picked a lock, although she'd once seen it done. Chad Owens, a boy she'd known in high school, had been showing off for the benefit of Nicole and a couple of her friends. It had taken him ten minutes to open the rusty padlock on the front door of a derelict house on their block that was rumored to be haunted. Once the door creaked open, the girls had refused to go in. After standing in the doorway for a good five minutes, even Chad had chickened out.

From that experience, she knew she'd need a second tool—a tension wrench—to use along with the lock pick. That she didn't have. Instead, she'd have to break a window. She picked up the biggest rock she could find and began the long climb up the stairs.

She was almost to the top before she saw that the window in the door was too high. Even if she managed to break it, there was no way she'd be able to reach the doorknob inside to unlock it.

She retreated downstairs, tossed the rock into the weeds, and went to the side of the house. She began trudging up the steep hill the house was built into. She'd gone just a short distance when she tripped over something and almost fell. When she turned on her flashlight, its glow revealed what had been invisible in the dark. Cement stepping stones were set into the hillside alongside the house. They were irregularly spaced, to all appearances a do-it-yourself project, and she had to keep the flashlight on all the way up. The beam grew dimmer as she climbed. By the time she reached the top, it had gone out altogether.

The house backed onto an empty lot that had been cleared of brush. A streetlight on the road above provided enough light for Nicole to see where she was going. After looking around, she found another good-sized rock and picked it up. She approached this door to the house and smacked the window with it. Most of the glass shattered and fell inside. Careful not to cut herself on the remaining shards, she reached in and unlocked the door.

# EIGHTEEN

ONCE NICOLE WAS INSIDE the house, she closed the door and locked it. Glancing up at the broken window, she realized she'd been silly to bother. The kidnappers had the key. Besides, once they spotted the shattered window, they'd know someone had broken in.

The lights on the street above provided enough illumination for her to see that she was in a kitchen. The air was musty and smelled of a combination of mildew and rancid cooking oil. The latter no doubt came from a big, ancient stove that loomed in one corner. Combined with these odors was a nasty undertone of something she couldn't identify. The smell compounded her sense of unease.

The kitchen was sparsely furnished, just a table and two chairs, along with the stove, which looked as if it hadn't been used in decades. Next to it was an equally old refrigerator, its door hanging by a single hinge.

Just then, she noticed a flashlight someone had left on the counter by the sink. She turned it on, took note of its nice, strong beam, and turned it off again. This would definitely come in handy. She pulled her gun out of her purse and dropped the flashlight in.

She held the gun in front of her as she started through the house. The next doorway led into what appeared to be the living room. It was sparsely furnished with just a metal TV stand and a dilapidated chair with stuffing leaking through its tattered upholstery. At one end of the room was a door. She opened it and found herself looking outdoors from the top of the front stairway. The view took in the yard, dark and utterly still. Beyond it, tree-covered hills were backlit by the glow of the city.

It didn't take long to go through the rest of the house. There were two small bedrooms. Each contained a single bedframe and springs, no mattress. She used the flashlight to investigate the closets. As far as she could see they were empty of everything but resident spiders and their webs.

She opened each door she passed. Next to the bedrooms, she found a tiny bathroom. As soon as she opened the door, she could tell this was the source of the stink she'd noticed when she walked in. It smelled as if something had died and been left to rot here. The shower curtain, opaque with mold, was pulled tight, hiding whatever was beyond it. With some trepidation, she pulled the curtain aside, got out her flashlight, and pointed the beam in the bathtub. To her relief, there was no dead rat or something she feared even more. Instead, the tub was black and crusty with a thick residue that emitted a terrible smell, probably from a sewage backup. When she left the bathroom, she closed the door, although the smell seemed to follow her as she circled back through the house, rechecking each dark corner and closet again. Convinced that no one was here, she put the gun in a pocket of her jacket.

She was disappointed to find no evidence that Steph had ever been in this house. The place looked as if it had been uninhabited for years. She hadn't found a door leading to the space under the house. Perhaps it wasn't a basement, just crawl space, accessible through an opening outside. Before she left, she'd have to find a way to see what was down there.

She was standing in the kitchen, trying to figure out what to do next, when she had an idea. Growing up, she and Steph had bedrooms that shared a wall. They had a secret signal that meant, "I can't sleep. Are you awake?" She kneeled on the floor and tapped it out: two knocks, a silence, then three more knocks and another silence, followed by a single knock. She jumped at the sound of footsteps coming from below. They grew louder, as if someone was climbing stairs. When they stopped, the signal was repeated back to her. The sound wasn't directly beneath her but from the direction of the kitchen.

Nicole's heart leapt at the sound, and she felt her eyes well up. Steph was here; she really was! "Steph," she called. "Where are you?"

"In the basement."

"How do I get to you? Is the entrance outside?"

"No. It's in the house somewhere. The door has a hole cut in it with a flap attached. When it's open, I can see into a hallway."

"I'll look around some more," Nicole said. She made another tour of the kitchen, using the flashlight to explore the dark corner next to the refrigerator. This illuminated a hallway she hadn't seen in her earlier search. The hall led to a service porch containing an ancient preautomatic washer. Its tub was round and capacious enough for commercial use, mounted on wheels so it could be rolled out of the way. Nevertheless, it was sitting in the center of the utility room, jutting out into the hallway. Next to it was a rusty step stool. She'd seen photos of washers like this but had never run across one in real life. It was an antique and, if it were in better shape, might have been worth something. But this one, like the kitchen appliances, was no more than junk. Its enamel finish had worn off, and the tub had several holes where rust had eaten through.

At the end of the hallway was a door that matched Steph's description. It had a hole cut in it. The flap that covered it was attached to the door at the bottom with hinges and a hook-and-eye latch at the top.

Nicole put her head against the door. "You there?"

"Right on the other side," Steph answered. "Can you get it open?"

Nicole tried the doorknob. "It's locked and there's no key." She studied the doorknob, which had a keyhole in the middle. It would be simple to open, if she had the tension wrench to go with her lock pick. It also would have helped if she actually remembered how it was done. Well, she thought, it was worth a try.

"I'll be right back," she said. "I'm going to see if I can find something to pick the lock."

There wasn't much in the kitchen cupboards, but one of the drawers yielded up a rusty paring knife with a fairly sharp point. Maybe this would do.

Nicole took it back to the basement door. "Hold tight," she told Steph. "I've got some tools that might work." She got down on her knees. Positioning the flashlight between her shoulder and neck, she managed to aim it so the beam fell on the doorknob. She stuck the pick into the lock and then the point of the knife, which she began to wiggle around. Nothing happened. Anxiety was making her hands shake. She had to free Steph and get her out of here before the kidnappers came back. She reversed the tools and jiggled them until she heard a loud click. Her first thought was that her efforts had paid off, and she'd managed to unlock the door. But when she pulled out the knife, she saw this hadn't happened. Instead, the knifepoint had broken off and was stuck in the lock.

At that moment, a hand gripped her shoulder while another was clamped over her mouth. She struggled to pull away, then bit down hard on the hand.

"Ow!" someone hissed in her ear. "It's me—Arnault. I covered your mouth so you wouldn't scream when I came up behind you." He released her and added, "We have to keep quiet. A car just pulled up on the street above. I don't know who's in it, but I think we'd better get out of here as soon as possible. Is your sister locked in here?"

"Yes. I tried to pick the lock. The point of the knife I was using broke off in it. I think it's hopeless."

He pulled a small flashlight out of his pocket, along with a leather case. From this, he took out tools she recognized as proper lock picks. "Here," he said, handing her the flashlight. "Shine the light on the doorknob."

As she did this, she said, "How did you find me?"

"I slipped a GPS device into your purse. That was why I dropped by your office twice today. I meant to do it in the morning, but your purse wasn't out, so I had to make a second visit."

"You planted a GPS on me? Is that even legal?"

"What? You're going to report me?" He gave a snort of laughter. By now, he'd extracted the knifepoint and was working on the lock. "I really do wish you'd listened to me and not come here on your own."

She didn't say anything. The fact was that she'd found Steph on her own, and she'd learned the whereabouts of the kidnappers, all on her own. She reached into her pocket for the grocery receipt where she'd written the address of the kidnapper's hideout. She handed it to Arnault and explained what it was.

"Wow!" he said. "Good work!" He quickly slipped it in his pocket and resumed working on the lock. A moment later, he managed to get the door open. Steph appeared and stumbled past him to throw her arms around Nicole. They both started to cry. After three days in someone else's dirty clothes, without access to soap, hot water, or deodorant, Steph smelled. Nicole didn't care, but when she put her cheek against Steph's she noticed how hot it was. Steph turned away to let out a croupy cough.

"You're sick!" Nicole said.

"A bit," Steph said. "Three days in that cold, damp basement."

Just then a car door slammed on the street above, and they heard the sound of men's voices. It was impossible to make out what they were saying, but they were getting louder as they approached the house.

Arnault gave Nicole a shove. "Quick! Hide. We can't let them find you. Once they do, it's all over. They'll force you to wire transfer the money and kill us all. Stephanie, go back downstairs."

Nicole looked around. The only possible hiding place was the big tub of the old washer. She used the step stool to hoist herself up and tumbled into the tub. She was surprised to find she still had her purse on her arm.

She could hear the men shouting just outside. In a flash, they were running through the kitchen into the hallway. They stopped at the doorway to the basement, just past where she was hiding.

She wondered where Arnault could be. Maybe he'd taken advantage of the darkness to blend into the shadows.

The men—there were two of them—seemed to think the basement door was still locked. "You know where the key is?" one of them said.

"Yeah," the other answered. "It's on the ledge above the door." Nicole recognized the voice. It was Kevin James from the bank. She'd had a hunch he might be involved, but hadn't really believed this polite, soft-spoken young man could be mixed up in kidnapping and murder.

"Hands up! Police!" It was Arnault, who had emerged from wherever he'd been hiding. There was a crashing sound; a gun went off, and there were sounds of a struggle.

Someone—she had a feeling it was Arnault—seemed to have been pushed down the basement stairs. She could hear him noisily tumbling down in what seemed like an endless series of thumps. The door was slammed behind him. Then everything went silent.

Nicole was still, holding her breath. Her heart was beating loudly in her throat, and she was shaking, trying to hold back the sobs bubbling up inside her.

"What the hell, Ryan?" Kevin said. "That fall could have killed him."

"So?" Ryan said. "We'd be getting rid of those two anyway."

"Says who?"

"Don't be so dense," Ryan said. "You know Ashley was never going to free Stephanie. The same goes for the cop." He was silent a moment before he said, "Hey," as if something had just occurred to him. "How do we know that guy didn't have a phone on him? He could call for backup. We need to search him when we go down to get the woman."

"Don't worry about his phone." Kevin's voice was soft, placating. "There's no signal up here, remember? That means he can't call anybody. Even if he managed to get out of the basement. We can make sure he can't go anywhere. I spotted a car parked on Kirkwood on our way up. It was way up on the curb, but the street's so narrow I had to slow down and inch around it. The street's plastered with no-parking signs. That car's got to be his. No one but a cop would park like that. We'll stop on the way out and make sure it's out of commission. Even if he manages to get out of the basement, he won't have any way to get help until we're long gone.

"Down to business," Kevin went on. "We're here for one reason—to get Stephanie and bring her back with us. Ashley wants to take her to the new hideout. Let's go down and get her."

"Wait," Ryan said. "What if that cop has an ankle holster with a second gun? If he's still on his feet, he could be waiting for us. We'll have to shove that washer aside so we can open the door all the way and have a clear view before we go down."

A moment later, Nicole felt the washing machine move, then start to roll. It hit the wall with a thud and ricocheted against something else. The impact threw Nicole off balance. Her head bumped against the tub, and she let out a cry.

Almost immediately, a flashlight was shining in her eyes, blinding her. Hands grabbed her and roughly pulled her out of the tub.

"Well, look what we've got here," Ryan said. Noticing the purse she was clutching, he snatched it away and dropped it on the floor. He turned to Kevin. "Open the basement door. We'll leave this one locked in the basement and take her sister back to Ashley."

"Wait," Nicole said. "Take me instead. All Ashley wants is my money, and I'm the only one who can get it for her. If I go with you now, we can get to the bank first thing in the morning."

"She has a point," Kevin said. "This will save time." He reached over to lock the basement door.

"Aren't we going to nail it shut?" Ryan said.

"No need. When we get done with that cop's car, the two of them are stuck here with no way to call for help."

Nicole was shaking with apprehension. Her gun was still in her pocket, and she was certain they'd search her and take it away. But somehow it didn't occur to Kevin or Ryan that she might be armed. They didn't bother looking in her pockets or patting her down. Instead, they each grabbed an arm and hustled her out of the house.

# NINETEEN

AFTER THE KIDNAPPERS LEFT with Nicole, Stephanie and Arnault lay in a dazed heap at the bottom of the basement stairs.

Arnault was the first to pull himself together, assess the situation, and get up. His left ankle gave out a burst of pain when he put his weight on it. But his main concern was Stephanie, who was breathing in short gasps. She'd been standing near the bottom of the steps when he fell, and he'd knocked her over, partially landing on her.

He bent over her. "Are you all right?" he said.

"I don't know." She spoke slowly in a semi-whisper, as if each word hurt. "I think I just got the wind knocked out of me"

He reached down to help her up. "Let's get you on your feet."

Steph started to extend her arm but quickly drew it back. "I can't. It hurts too much. I don't think I can get up."

Ignoring his own injury, Arnault lifted her and carried her to the bed. When he put her down, she cried out in pain.

"Where does it hurt?" Arnault said.

"My ribs. And every time I try to breathe, there's a shooting pain down my back." She let out a dry, hacking cough that made her fold up into a ball. "Oh, God, that hurt!"

Arnault was worried her lung might have collapsed when they fell. "I'm going upstairs to call an ambulance and find Nicole."

"Uh-huh," she breathed.

Holding onto the railing, he slowly made his way up. His ankle throbbed with every step, and he kept having to stop.

At the top, he tried his phone again. Still no luck. He banged on the door and shouted, "Nicole!" But there was no response. After repeating this several times, he got the pouch with his tools out of his pocket, kneeled on the top step, and went to work on the lock. It was seconds before he stood up. "I've got the door unlocked," he called down to Stephanie. "I'll be right back."

Stephanie didn't answer, or if she did, he couldn't hear her.

In the laundry room, he checked the washer, not surprised to find it empty. Limping through the house, he called "Nicole!" while keeping an eye on his phone, which still had no signal. Nor was there any trace of Nicole. It was his worst fear. The kidnappers had taken her. All at once, he remembered the slip of paper she'd handed him before she climbed into the washer. He went through his pockets until he found it. The address she'd written was in the Melrose district of Hollywood. She'd said this was where the kidnappers were holed up. They'd probably taken her there. He had to get some squad cars to that address.

But his first priority was Stephanie. A collapsed lung was serious; it could be fatal. He went outside and tried the phone again. Still the same "no service" message in tiny letters at the top of the screen. Cell phone service was always spotty in the canyons. If he couldn't get a signal here, he'd have to go down to his car and drive around until he could connect.

First, he returned to the basement door, which he'd left standing open. He didn't think he could climb down the stairs and back up again. Instead, he pulled his flashlight out of his pocket and pointed the beam into the basement so he could see

Stephanie.

"I can't find Nicole," he called, "and my phone won't work from here. I have to get you an ambulance and send squad cars to an address where they might find Nicole. I don't want to leave you here alone. Is there any chance you can get up the stairs if you lean on me?"

She looked up at him and shook her head, then put it down again, apparently too short of breath to answer.

"Okay," he said. "I'll be back as soon as I make these calls."

Once outside he used the flashlight to search the yard, hoping to find something sturdy to take his weight off his injured ankle. He was in luck. A dead fruit tree near the fence had dropped several branches. He selected the sturdiest one and broke off twigs near one end to make it easier to hold. He hobbled to the side of the house and started the steep trek downhill to where he'd parked.

# TWENTY

ONCE THE CAR STARTED UP, the two men were silent. Nicole sat quietly in the back seat. They drove downhill, rounded a sharp curve, and stopped in front of a car that was parked on the shoulder of the road.

The men got out without closing the doors. Nicole couldn't see what they were doing, but wasn't long before they were back. When the car started up again, they began to talk as if they'd forgotten Nicole was there.

"About that cop," Ryan said, "I don't like it. He saw our faces. We should have killed him."

"Don't you get it?" Kevin said. "That would make us cop killers."

"So what? They already think we killed Rexton, even though it was his own fault. What a loser! He was so out of shape that when he took a swing at me, he fell down, hit his head, and knocked himself out." Ryan barked a laugh. "And when they find Victoria Reina in the freezer, guess what? They'll pin that on us, too, even though we had nothing to do with it."

"It doesn't matter," Kevin said. "Kidnapping with bodily harm means life in prison. As for killing a cop, nothing makes the police madder than if you kill one of them. It's like a cop's life is worth twenty of ours. You'd better hope that guy survived the fall. If he's dead, and they catch us, we'll end up on death row. That's why we have to focus on getting the rest of Nicole's money and leaving the country before they're onto us."

"Can't they extradite us?" Ryan said.

"No way," Kevin said. "Ashley got us fake passports with new identities. Besides, we're going to Nicaragua. They don't extradite."

"I still don't like it," Ryan growled. "And I don't trust Ashley. She's a con artist and a liar. She got us into this mess. First, she gets Matt on board by acting like he's her new boyfriend. Then she promises us big money for a simple kidnapping scam. Before we know it, we're in deep with two deaths and three kidnappings, including Ashley's. And now she claims she can only pay us forty thousand dollars each because she didn't get the millions in ransom she thought her husband was going to pay. You know what? I'll bet she doesn't plan to pay us anything.

"Notice how she kept her own hands clean?" he ranted. "You know what? I'm not even going to mention that cop to her. If she hears he was snooping around, she'll run out and leave us holding the bag."

Nicole was keeping track of the car's route. It wasn't long before she could tell they were headed for the courtyard apartment south of Melrose.

At last the car stopped. Kevin got out and opened the door for her. He spoke in a low voice so Ryan couldn't hear. "Ashley's a little harsh. Just stay cool. As soon as the bank opens, we'll take you there. You'll wire the money into our account. The minute the deposit is confirmed, we'll let you and your sister go."

"What about the cop you threw down the basement steps?"

"I wasn't the one who did that. But he'll be released, too. I promise."

Nicole doubted that even Kevin believed this. From what she'd just overheard, it was clear no decision had been made about Arnault. In any case, she could see that Kevin had no say in what was going to happen. Ashley was in charge. Nicole knew she'd have to figure out how to get away from these people before morning. She, Arnault, and perhaps even Steph had seen the kidnappers' faces and could identify them. How could they risk letting them go?

By now, Ryan had come around from the driver's side. "What are you two talking about?" Ryan turned to Kevin. "Get it through your head that she's not your friend. The minute she has a chance, she'll turn you in." Then, to Nicole, "Get out of the car and come with us. If you scream or try to get away, you'll be sorry. Got that?"

Nicole nodded. She climbed out of the car and walked between the two men as they headed toward bungalow No. 5.

The men stood back to let Nicole enter first. The place was even smaller than it appeared from outside. The décor looked like it had been lifted from a 1930s movie set: two old-fashioned overstuffed chairs, each with a doily; a small love seat; a somewhat battered upright piano with a cheap, imitation Hummel shepherd on top. Lace curtains completed the effect. The air was stuffy and smelled of leftovers. Discarded food containers were piled in one corner.

Matt was already there, stretched out on the love seat with his legs dangling over the end. His arm was in a cast, and he looked miserable.

As they entered, Ryan took Nicole's arm and guided her to the love seat. "Move over," he told Matt. Matt gave Ryan a resentful look but did what he said. Ryan looked at Nicole and pointed to the love seat. "Sit," he said. He and Kevin took the two chairs.

"What's she doing here?" Matt said. "Where's Stephanie?"

"This bitch turned up at the house," Ryan said. "We left the sister locked in the basement and brought this one instead. It makes things easier."

Matt scowled, as if he didn't follow Ryan's logic. "Whatever," he said. "But what's happened to Ashley? She's supposed to be here by now. Do you think she ran out on us?"

"Don't be a dumbass," Ryan said. "She's not going anywhere until we get the money from what's-her-name here."

Matt nodded. "Right."

They sat in tense silence, waiting for Ashley to arrive. None of the men seemed in a mood to talk. Instead, they eyed each other with what appeared to be suspicion and resentment, as if they'd had a falling out. Nicole wondered what this was about and whether she could use it to her advantage. She glanced at her watch. It was two o'clock in the morning. She figured a half hour must have passed since they left the house. Another half hour went by before there was a knock on the door.

Kevin got up and pulled the front window curtain aside to peek out. When he opened the door, a woman walked in. Nicole had seen the photo of the disguised Ashley on Matt's Facebook page. Now she'd taken on a completely different appearance. Instead of the wild, dark curls, Ashley's hair, now dyed brown, was mannishly short and spikey. Devoid of makeup, she looked just like Jessica Reese in the mugshot taken six years ago. The tight-fitting designer clothes had been replaced by a tired-looking loose jacket, which she wore with baggy jeans, Birkenstocks, and thick gray socks. She looked as if she'd tried to appear as unchic as possible and had succeeded brilliantly. The biggest surprise came when Ashley took off the jacket. The woman was pregnant, perhaps six months along. Nicole wondered why no one had bothered to mention this.

Ashley frowned at Nicole, as if she found her presence an affront. "What's she doing here? Where's Stephanie?"

Once again Ryan explained their decision to bring Nicole instead of her sister. "This means we can go to the bank first thing tomorrow morning and have her wire the money."

"Take her to the bank?" Ashley said. "You've got to be kidding! Look at her. Her clothes are dirty, her hair's a mess, and she's got leaves in it. What did you do to her?"

"Nothing," Ryan seemed cowed by Ashley's tone. "I mean, she was like that when we found her. She was hiding in a big washtub. We lifted her out and brought her here."

"She can't go anywhere looking like that." Ashley turned to Kevin. "Why can't you go into the bank and do the wire transfer yourself? We'll make her give us her account number and password. Just go into work at the usual time and take care of it."

"Wait!" Nicole said. "I don't have my account number or password with me."

Ashley scowled at Nicole, as if incensed that she had the nerve to interrupt. Ashley then turned back to Kevin. "You can look up her account and do the transfer, right?"

"Not really," Kevin said, "I mean, I could look it up, but I don't have her password or the authority to make a transfer that large if the account holder isn't there to sign the forms. If I tried, it would be a red flag for the manager, who considers Nicole some kind of rock star, especially since all that money turned up in her account. He'd know something was going on."

There was a pause while Ashley fumbled under the back of her tunic, which was stretched across her belly. A moment later, she pulled off a fake, plastic baby bump and dropped it on the floor. Wordlessly, she pointed to Ryan's chair. He got up, and she flopped down on it, as if exhausted. "Whoosh," she said. "That thing is so uncomfortable! Remind me never to get pregnant." She turned to Nicole, addressing her directly for the first time. "All right. Where is your banking information? At your place? I'll send one of these useless dicks to get it."

Nicole paused, thinking carefully what to say. The truth was that she'd memorized the information, and it was in her head. "My password's on a card in my wallet," she said. "It's in my purse, along with my checkbook, which has my account number. Ryan took my purse when we were at the house."

Ashley turned to Ryan. "Is that true? You've got her purse?"

"Uh—no. Like she said. I thought she might have a cell phone in there, so I took it. I meant to bring it along, but—"

"You total screw-up!" Ashley could hardly contain her anger. "Well—what did you do with it?"

He shook his head. "I must have set it down somewhere."

"At the house on Kirkwood?"

"Yeah."

"Go back and get it. Now!" Ashley snapped. "And step on it! We've got to get out of here before the cops find us."

# TWENTY ONE

ARNAULT'S CAR DROVE SMOOTHLY for the first block or so. After that, it began to wobble, the wheels making thumping sounds, as if he was driving over boulders. He stopped, got out, and used the flashlight to inspect the tires. With a sinking heart, he saw that that all of them, front and rear, were completely flat. That the car was his would have been obvious to the kidnappers. It was the only one in the no-parking zone on the narrow street. They must have noticed it and slashed the tires in case he escaped from the basement. It occurred to him that Nicole must have driven up here, but he didn't see her car. Perhaps she'd parked on the street above the house. But he couldn't waste time looking for it.

He sighed. He'd told Stephanie he'd be back in a few minutes, but finding a phone signal was going to take longer—perhaps a lot longer. He was glad he had the tree branch to take his weight off his injured ankle. He'd have to keep going until he found a spot where his cell would connect. If he reached Laurel Canyon and still couldn't call, he might be able to flag down a motorist who'd drive him down to Sunset, which was well populated with phone towers. Meanwhile, he had no way to let Stephanie know where he was.

Arnault slowly made his way down the steep grade of Kirkwood Drive. Even with the walking stick, the pain in his ankle was hard to ignore. He figured it must be a sprain. Logic told him that if his ankle was broken, he wouldn't have been able to walk at all. He began to hop along, using the walking stick to avoid putting his foot down. But this was exhausting. His pace was slow, and he stopped once in a while to check his phone. It was a good half hour before he finally reached Laurel Canyon Boulevard, and the phone still didn't work. Nor were any cars in sight. The houses along the winding road were dark. He figured his only choice was to turn right and head down toward Sunset Boulevard.

After a few blocks, he sensed a light behind him and turned to see a car coming down the hill. He stepped out into the approaching vehicle's path and waved his arms. Without slowing, the car veered around him. The driver leaned on the horn and roared his engine as he passed, as if enraged that someone would have the nerve to try to delay him.

Arnault started walking again. When he couldn't go any farther, he hobbled to the side of the road and sat on the curb. He leaned back on his elbows and closed his eyes. He dozed for a bit. When he woke, he had no idea how much time had passed. He got up and began limping downhill again. A block passed, then another, and he kept going. At last he spotted headlights in the distance. This vehicle was heading up the hill from Sunset. As it drew closer, he stepped into the road and waved his arms. The car skidded to a stop a few feet away.

The driver lowered his window a couple of inches and shouted, "What the hell, dude? You trying to commit suicide? I almost ran you down."

By now Arnault was holding his badge up. "Police," he said. "I had to leave a seriously injured woman up the hill. I need you to drive me to where I can pick up a phone signal and call an ambulance."

The man put on his safety blinkers and hopped out of the car. Only when he came into the glare of the headlights did Arnault see this was one of the kidnappers, the same one who'd shoved him down the stairs. He was holding a gun that Arnault recognized as his own.

Ryan grabbed Arnault's walking stick and tossed it away. Then he forced Arnault around to the back of the vehicle, making him climb into the rear seat with his hands behind his back. Ryan tied his hands together. He gave Arnault a thump on the side of his head with the gun. "Lie on your stomach," he commanded.

Arnault did as he said. Before he realized what was happening, his ankles were tied tightly together, compounding the pain in the injured one. The back door of the SUV was slammed shut, and the vehicle started up again.

They went a short distance before Ryan parked. He untied Arnault and pulled him out of the car. Only now did Arnault see they'd returned to the house where he'd left Stephanie and were parked on the street above the back entrance. Arnault was forced into the house at gunpoint. When Ryan opened the door to the basement, Arnault tensed up, expecting to be shoved down the stairs again. Instead, Ryan used his flashlight to light the way, allowing Arnault to limp down slowly, leaning on the railing.

Ryan descended just far enough to be sure Stephanie was still there. He climbed back up, closed the door and relocked it. He located a hammer and nails in a laundry room cupboard and nailed the the basement door shut again. Satisfied that this would keep the cop contained, he tossed the hammer aside. He picked up Nicole's purse from the hall floor, where he'd dropped it earlier. Mission accomplished, he left, slamming the back door without bothering to lock it.

# TWENTY-TWO

AFTER RYAN LEFT THE COURTYARD apartment, Ashley also headed out. "I'm going to find an all-night drugstore," she said. "I need a hairdryer and supplies to make Nicole look like someone with legitimate reason to walk into a bank."

Nicole sat quietly on her side of the love seat, trying not to call attention to herself. She was thinking about her next move. By some miracle, her gun had gone unnoticed and was still in her pocket. But she knew it would be unwise to take on both men at once. Divide and conquer, she thought. She didn't have any real plan—just a tentative list of possibilities. She'd have to improvise as she went along.

Matt was hunkered down on his end of the love seat with his legs stretched out in front of him. His eyes were closed, although he didn't seem to be asleep. He kept shifting about and moaning as if his arm was causing a lot of pain. Kevin was standing near the window, fiddling with his phone. The two men had spoken briefly about getting pizza delivered, and Kevin seemed to be taking a long time completing the order.

Nicole got to her feet. "I have to use the bathroom," she said.

Kevin looked up and turned to Matt. "Hey, dude," he said. "Keep an eye on her. I'm busy here."

Matt moaned as he slowly pulled himself to his feet and followed Nicole to the bathroom. She was surprised when he allowed her to shut the door all the way. The single window over the tub was too small for her to climb out of, even if she could reach it. She quietly stepped into the tub and slid the window open. She got out and adjusted the shower curtain so it completely covered the tub. Finally, she took the key out of the lock, put it in her pocket, and pulled out her gun. She positioned herself against the wall so she'd be hidden when the door opened.

She waited at least fifteen minutes before Matt said, "Hey! What's taking so long in there?" He knocked on the door several times before entering. Once open, the door hid Nicole without bouncing back and closing as she'd feared. She could hear Matt moving around in the tiny bathroom, mumbling to himself. The shower curtain crinkled as he pulled it out of the way. A couple of hollow thuds followed, as he stepped into the tub, presumably to look out the window.

By the time he turned around, Nicole was pointing the gun at him. He put his hands up in surrender, his face registering shock and fear.

Nicole spoke in a low voice so Kevin couldn't hear over the blare of the TV. "I'm going to lock you in here. If you yell or make a fuss, I'll shoot through the door. Even if I miss you, people in the other units will hear and call the police."

"Don't lock me in here!" Matt pleaded. "Ashley will kill us if we let you escape. She's a sociopath. I'm telling you, she's brutal."

"Don't worry about Ashley," Nicole said. "Before she gets back, Kevin will realize you've been gone too long and let you out." She walked out of the bathroom, locked the door with the key she'd taken from inside, and put it back in her pocket. She was fairly confident that Matt wouldn't be able to kick the door in. Old as these bungalows were, they were solidly built.

The next step was to neutralize Kevin. It wasn't hard. All she had to do was walk into the living room and point the gun at him. He offered no resistance. Instead, his face turned red and crumpled, as if he were about to cry.

"Nicole!" His voice was shaky. "I'm your friend, remember? I've been on your side from the start. I made sure nobody hurt you."

She did feel a little sorry for him. He'd been duped into this, like the others. Ashley had promised a big payoff to these inexperienced and unprincipled losers. They had no way of knowing how badly things would turn out. But, she thought, if you dance to the tune, you have to pay the piper. If she let Kevin go, he was sure to call Ryan and Ashley and warn them to stay away. And no matter what, Kevin wouldn't walk away free. Ryan and Matt would point the finger at him the minute they were arrested.

She noticed a set of keys on the coffee table. "Are those your car keys?"

"I don't have a car. They're Matt's. What did you do with him?"

She ignored his question. "You're going to pick up those keys and hand them to me, along with your cell phone. Then you'll show me where Matt parked his car. We'll walk out together just like we'd normally do, except I'll have this gun pointed at you. Don't try anything."

Silently, Kevin nodded as tears ran down his face.

"And stop crying. I'll tell the police you tried to protect me," she said. "I'm sure they'll cut you a break, especially if you offer to testify against the others. Just explain one thing to me. Why three kidnappings? Why didn't Ashley simply arrange for you to kidnap her if her goal was to get money from her husband's trust fund?"

"We wondered about that," Kevin said. "At first, she told us these other women were friends who'd gotten together to set up fake kidnappings to get money out of their husbands. We figured, 'Okay, the women were in on it, and the husbands probably deserved it.' But when we took the first victim, she acted really scared, like she wasn't expecting it. We asked Ashley about it, and she said the woman was just pretending. Next time, Victoria Reina fought like a wildcat when we took her. We said we knew she and her friends had planned the whole thing. When we mentioned Ashley's name, she said Ashley was no friend of hers, and she'd never made any such plan. Then Victoria ended up dead, which totally freaked us out. We told Ashley to tell us the truth or we wouldn't go through with the kidnapping she'd planned for herself."

By now, Nicole and Kevin had reached Matt's car, an ancient Volvo. They got in, Nicole in the driver's seat, still pointing her gun at Kevin who'd settled on the passenger's side. "Go on," she prompted. "What did Ashley say?"

"You have to understand about Ashley," he said. "She's usually pretty unpleasant, but when she wants to, she puts on charm. She can be pretty convincing. Sometimes, what she says doesn't make sense when you think about it later. But at the time, she has you totally believing her. That's why she's so great at conning people."

"And—?"

"She said nobody kidnaps adults for ransom in the U.S. any more—like, practically ever. It's big in third world countries. And her father-in-law, who controlled her husband's money, was already suspicious of her. That's why her own kidnapping had to look like part of a crime wave. You know, kidnappers targeting rich people in L.A. She set the ransom low so the victims would be quick to pay and unlikely to call the police if we told them we'd do something drastic if they did. We'd be in and out in a couple of days. Then she planned to up the ante with her own kidnapping. Like the first two were just practice for the big score. It kind of makes sense."

"It would stop making sense when she asked for ten million

dollars," Nicole said. "That's a lot different than fifty thousand dollars. Thanks for explaining, Kevin." She waved the gun at him. "I can't drive and hold a gun on you at the same time. Stay where you are until I come around to open your door."

He stared at her, looking hopeful. "Are you letting me go?"

Instead of answering, she hopped out of the car and circled in front with the gun still trained on him. She opened the door and told Kevin to get out. She marched him to the rear of the car and opened the trunk, using the flashlight to make sure the car was too old to have an interior trunk release. Satisfied he wouldn't be able to escape, she ordered Kevin to climb in.

This made him start crying in earnest. She shushed him. "Please let me go," he said in a loud whisper. "I'll disappear. No one will ever hear from me again."

She waved the gun at him. "I offered you a deal like that at the house. Remember? Too bad you didn't take it. Get in."

Snuffling loudly, he climbed in. Nicole closed the trunk. She needed to call the police, but first she had to put some distance between herself and the courtyard bungalow. Ashley might be back any minute. Nicole got in the driver's seat and headed east toward Melrose Avenue. After-hours clubs would still be open, and people would be out walking. On the way, she had to pull over because Kevin was crying loudly, begging for mercy. She got out and thumped on the trunk several times, warning him, "Shut up or I'll shoot you." He immediately grew silent.

Once she was safely parked on Melrose, she called 911, asking for the Robbery-Homicide team working on the Rexton kidnapping. After a bit of explaining, she was connected. She told the officer who answered that Arnault was being held prisoner at the house on Kirkwood and might be injured. She gave him that address, as well as the one for the bungalow where Ryan had taken her. This accomplished, she made a U-turn and headed back to Laurel Canyon.

By the time she arrived on Kirkwood, the house was

surrounded by police cars, as well as paparazzi on motorbikes and several news vans. She had to park a couple of blocks away and walk up the hill. The front of the property was marked off with yellow crime-scene tape. She was about to duck under it when a burly cop walked over. "This is a crime scene." He gestured toward the tape. "You can't enter the property." She explained that she was the one who'd called 911 and that her kidnapped sister was inside.

"You heard me," the cop was gruff and impatient. "Move on!"

"My sister's in there," she repeated. "I have to make sure she's all right."

"You just have to wait over there with everyone else." Then he added, "Sorry." But he didn't look sorry. His expression was as sour as when he'd first walked up to her.

She considered turning Kevin over to him but quickly decided against it. Not only did the cop not believe her, he seemed to have taken a dislike to her. Maybe he thought she was a reporter.

She remembered the way the yard was laid out with trees and bushes blocking the view of the house. She could cut through the neighboring yard and stay hidden behind the foliage. She walked downhill to the next overgrown lot and then up again. Keeping behind the trees and bushes, she managed to get to her destination without being seen. As she started up the steep path beside the house, she wondered if Steph and Arnault were still in the house. Maybe they'd already been taken away by the police or, in Arnault's case, an ambulance. Just then she heard a siren and figured she'd made it in time.

It was still dark although the sky was just beginning to lighten. When she reached the top of the hill, she peeked around the corner. Four big cops were standing near the road that ran behind the house. They had their backs to her and were busy keeping a small crowd of paparazzi and other media types out of the yard. More TV news vans were parked across the street, and a news helicopter was circling overhead. As the siren of the ambulance grew louder, the cops got into their squad cars to move them out of the way. While they were occupied, Nicole made a run for the back door and slipped inside.

She was immediately stopped by a plain-clothes detective who was standing in the middle of the kitchen. He was tall and somewhat heavy with steel gray hair and glasses to match. "Whoa," he said. "How'd you get in? You have to leave."

"I'm Nicole Graves," she said, "I'm the kidnap victim's sister. I have to see her."

"Oh, yeah," said the detective, suddenly conciliatory. "You're the one who called and tipped us off about this place. Sure, just sit over there." He gestured to the corner that held the table and two chairs. "You'll be out of the way when the paramedics come in to bring your sister and Detective Arnault up from the basement. By the way, I'm Joe Hammon. Arnault told me about you."

He held out his hand to shake hers, but she was too busy processing what he'd just said to notice. "Oh, my God!" she said. "Is Steph hurt? Is it serious?"

"Arnault was thrown down the stairs. Your sister happened to be standing near the bottom. He knocked her down and partly landed on her. She's having trouble breathing. We'll know more when the paramedics have a look."

A door banged open behind Nicole, and four paramedics rushed into the house. They were carrying two portable stretchers and backboards. Nicole was in a panic. How badly was Steph hurt? And what about Arnault?

"Did Ryan ever show up?" she asked Hammon, once the paramedics had disappeared down the stairs. "He's one of the kidnappers. Earlier, he took me to a bungalow apartment south of Melrose. He was supposed to come back here to get my purse. I told them it contained my banking information."

"You mean you were kidnapped, too?"

"Not exactly," she said. "I persuaded them to take me instead of my sister."

"Same thing," he said. "I'll need to get your statement. As for Ryan Holich, yes. We caught him just as he was leaving the house. He's handcuffed in one of cruisers up there." He nodded his head toward the street above. "You know, he did have a purse with him. We bagged it as evidence. I'm afraid you'll have to wait until it goes through the process before we can return it."

"How long will that take?"

"It could take a while," Hammon said. "I'll do my best to expedite it."

Nicole thought about what was in her purse. Her main concern was her beloved cell phone; she used it so much, it was like was like an extension of her hand. Fortunately, she'd left it home, along with her car keys. By another stroke of luck, Daniel, the Uber driver, had taken her wallet with her credit cards; she could get those back in the morning. And she'd put her drivers' license along with Daniel's phone information and his car keys in the pocket of her jeans. Her gun was in her coat pocket, where she'd put it after forcing Kevin into the trunk. As it turned out, her purse wasn't that big of a loss.

"Did you find anyone at the bungalow apartment?" she said.

"Just one person, a Matthew—" he consulted his notepad, "Bissell. He was arrested. They're taking him down to the station."

"A woman was involved, too," she said. "Ashley Knowles."

"Ashley Knowles?" He sounded puzzled. "She was the last kidnap victim."

"Not really," Nicole said. "She masterminded the whole thing to get at her husband's trust fund." She explained about Ashley's involvement. Then she said, "When I saw her earlier, she was wearing a pretty effective disguise."

The paramedics reappeared with Stephanie on a stretcher. She seemed to be barely breathing. Nicole grabbed her sister's hand, but Steph didn't respond.

"Please," Nicole said to the paramedic who seemed to be in charge. "This is my sister. You have to let me go in the ambulance with her."

"I'm sorry," he said. "That's not allowed. We're heading for Cedars. You can follow in your car."

"Can you tell me anything about her injury?"

"I'm not a doctor, but she's having trouble breathing. We have to get her to the hospital STAT."

Nicole hurried along beside the stretcher, grasping Steph's hand, until they reached the ambulance. She had to let go when they loaded the stretcher in. As they did, Steph began to cough and gasp for breath. She was so pale she was almost blue.

Nicole repeated her request to ride along. "Please! She looks like she's dying. I'm her only family."

"Sorry," the paramedic repeated. "I can't. It's policy." As he closed the back of the vehicle, one of the other paramedics donned a face mask and gloves and started working on Steph.

"I'll get the car," Nicole said.

Detective Hammon placed his hand on Nicole's shoulder. "I'm afraid you can't leave quite yet. We have to get your statement and, most important, a description of Ashley Rexton's disguise, since the police haven't found her yet. Meanwhile, your sister is in good hands. Come with me. We can sit in one of the squad cars." Reluctantly, Nicole followed him up to the street where the vehicles were parked.

All at once, she remembered that Kevin was still in the trunk of Matt's car, parked down the hill. She explained this to Hammon, told him where Matt's Volvo was parked, and handed him the keys. He summoned a uniformed cop and told him where to find the car. "Pop the trunk and cuff the man who's locked in there. Then drive him up here."

Hammon turned back to Nicole. "We'll need to impound the car because it was involved in a crime. But I'll drive you to the hospital after I take your statement. I need to go there anyway to debrief Arnault."

Nicole was suddenly aware of tears spilling down her face.

She started to use her sleeve to wipe them away, but the detective silently handed her a packet of Kleenex. At that moment, two more paramedics passed, bearing Arnault on a stretcher. His face was smudged with dirt, his clothes were filthy, and he was obviously in pain. Even so, he appeared to be in much better shape than Stephanie.

"Hey," Nicole said.

"Wait a second," Arnault said, and the paramedics stopped. "They say I may have a sprained ankle or it could be a hairline fracture," he said. "It looks like your sister has a collapsed lung, so she needs immediate treatment. They'll get right on it. She should be fine."

The paramedics started moving again, carrying Arnault to the remaining ambulance.

Hammon led Nicole to where the patrol cars were parked. As they passed the first one, she noticed movement inside. A moment later, Ryan pressed his face against the rear passenger window and shouted, "You bitch! I'm going to get you!"

Hammon went back and opened the front door of the vehicle. "Shut up," he said. "Or I'll add threatening a witness to the long list of charges against you." This had an instant effect. Ryan's expression went neutral. With his head down, he moved away from the window.

As Nicole climbed into the next squad car with Hannon, she realized she had to tell David about Stephanie's rescue and that she'd been injured and was on her way to the hospital. She pulled the phone out of her pocket and stared at it a moment, realizing it belonged to Kevin. The police would no doubt consider it evidence, but first she had to make this call. She explained to Hammon that she had to notify Steph's fiancé that she'd been rescued. When she called David's cell, he didn't pick up, so she left a message.

When she was done, she handed the phone to Hammon. "This belongs to one of the kidnappers. I guess you'll want it as evidence."

Hammon raised an eyebrow as he took it from her and produced a plastic evidence bag from the glove compartment. After he'd bagged the phone and put it in his pocket, he turned to Nicole and said, "Why don't you tell me everything that happened since you left home yesterday evening."

§

Nicole arrived at the hospital's emergency ward just in time to see Stephanie being wheeled out of a curtained cubicle.

No doctor was in sight, so she waylaid a passing nurse. "That's my sister they're taking away. I need to talk to whoever's treating her and find out about her condition."

The nurse took Nicole's name, as well as Stephanie's, and directed her to the waiting room. It was packed, and she ended up sitting on the floor. There she remained, her legs growing stiff while she watched the door from which doctors occasionally emerged to talk to those waiting. After about forty-five minutes, a young-looking woman in a white coat came out and called her name. When Nicole waved and stood up, the doctor gestured her to a corner where they could talk. The doctor, whose name tag said "Alice Chang, M.D." wore thick glasses. Her hair was pulled into bun.

"I understand that your sister had a fall. She sustained a broken rib. This, in turn, penetrated her lung, causing it to collapse. We've taken some temporary measures to help her breathe while we get her ready for surgery. We'll repair the damage to her lung and remove air from her chest cavity so the lung can reinflate."

"Will she be all right?" Nicole said.

"This operation is generally successful. Barring complications, she's going to be fine."

This failed to calm Nicole. "What complications?"

"Any surgery has risks, and your sister does have bronchitis, which complicates things a bit. But we already have her on a strong antibiotic. I think the outlook is excellent." Dr. Chang's voice was reassuring. "Try not to worry. This shouldn't take too long. We'll let you know as soon as she goes into recovery."

Nicole found a nearby restroom. As she was washing her hands, she looked at herself in the mirror and was shocked by her appearance. Her face was smudged with dirt, as was her jacket. Looking down, she could see her jeans were dirty, too. Her hair was a mess and really did have leaves in it, as Ashley had pointed out. Without her purse, Nicole had no comb or lipstick. She washed her face and dried it on a paper towel, then finger-combed her hair, pulling out the leaves. Finally, she brushed the dirt from her clothes as best she could.

When she was done, she returned to the waiting room to find David there, seated in one of the plastic chairs. He didn't smile, nor did he get up to give her his usual hug. He didn't look well at all. She sat down next to him and repeated what the doctor had said about Stephanie.

"And what about you?" Nicole said. "How are you feeling?"

"Not that great," he said. "I'm still a bit dizzy, and it upsets my stomach. The docs tell me it will take a month to six weeks before I'm back to my old self. But I'll get there." He gave a weary smile. "The important thing is that Steph is safe."

She could see he wasn't in a mood to talk. They sat in silence for what seemed like an eternity. She was about to check her watch when Arnault limped in wearing the kind of walking boot used for foot and ankle injuries. He was looking around for her.

She gave him a wave. He limped over to her, greeted David, then sat down next to her. They'd cleaned him up a bit, but he was still disheveled, wearing the same dirty clothes.

"They let you out?" she said.

"Yeah. It's just a sprain, although it hurts like hell. All they could do was tape it up, give me this stupid boot and some pain pills. How's your sister?'"

"She's in surgery. They said it wouldn't take long, but," she stopped and glanced at her watch, "it's been over an hour. I heard they caught Ryan and Matthew. And I was able to deliver Kevin to them. What's the latest on Ashley?"

"She got away," he said. "They have an APB out on her."

"I just hope she isn't using a new disguise," Nicole said. "And even if she doesn't have money to get out of the country, she's great at conning her way into wealthy people's lives. I wonder if you'll ever find her."

"We will," Arnault said. "Sooner or later."

At that moment, Dr. Chang appeared at the front desk and motioned Nicole over. Both David and Arnault followed. Chang smiled. "Stephanie came through beautifully. She's in recovery. It may be a little while before we find her a bed. As soon as we do, you'll be able to see her."

When Dr. Chang was gone, Nicole glanced at her watch. It was seven thirty a.m., late enough to call Daniel, the Uber driver. She borrowed Arnault's phone and reached Daniel on her first try. She explained, as briefly as she could, what had happened and where he could find his car. Fortunately, he had a spare key.

"If you see any dents or scratches, let me know," she said. "I'll take care of it. I'll call later and we'll figure out a convenient way for me to return your key and pick up my wallet. And thanks so much for the use of your car. You saved my sister's life and helped the police catch some really bad people."

"Wow!" Daniel said. "I had no idea. I mean, I'm glad I could be of help. Am I going to read about you in the news?"

Nicole hadn't thought of this. "I certainly hope not." She thanked him again, and they said goodbye.

All at once, she felt elated. Everything was taken care of. Steph was safe, and their troubles were over.

At that moment, Arnault got up. "I have to get back to the station," he said, "There's a load of paperwork to finish before we can close out this case."

"Sure," Nicole said. She felt a little let down. Would she ever see him again? Probably not. As he walked away, she realized it was for the best. There had been a definite vibe between then, but given her last experience with a cop, she knew it would go nowhere.

# Epilogue

The day was warm and sunny. Nicole was feeling especially upbeat when she arrived at the Polo Lounge for lunch with Sue. Today was their first chance to reschedule celebration of Nicole's bequest. Since then, Sue had been tied up in a long trial, and Nicole had been busy at work and occupied helping her sister get back on her feet. As for Nicole, she was still struggling to make peace with two million dollars that had caused them so much grief.

She was ten minutes late. As she looked around for Sue, she couldn't help remembering what was to be a celebratory breakfast two months before. It felt as if years had passed. A lot had happened since David's desperate call had sent her racing home just as the waitress arrived with the meal they'd ordered.

She found Sue waiting at a table overlooking the garden. With her cloud of red curls and delicate beauty, Sue could have been mistaken for a movie actress. As Nicole sat down across from her friend, she realized lunch was a better time for celebrity sightings at the Polo Lounge than breakfast. Seated at a long table behind Sue were the film megastar Hattie Longelle and her entourage. Nicole couldn't help glancing at them every time a burst of laughter came from that table. She hadn't seen any security guards in front of the hotel or near the restaurant's entrance. She wondered how they managed to keep out paparazzi and looky-loos.

"You could take the view that your inheritance is cursed," Sue was saying. "It certainly caused you enough trouble. But you have to stop regarding it as Robert Blair's dirty money and think of all the good it can do. You told me you wanted to get rid of it by making a one-time gift to Doctors Without Borders or The Homeless Project, but as time passes, the charities you feel passionate about will change. If you keep the money and it produces income, you'll be able to continue being a benefactor for a long time. It will also be there in case you or Steph need a cushion to fall back on."

Nicole nodded, pulling her eyes away from Hattie's table and back to Sue. "You're right," she said. As she knew too well, anything could happen. And if the world came crashing down on their heads, it would be good to have something in reserve. But she also knew that money wasn't the answer to every problem.

As she considered how the money could be used, she thought of the ancient Toyota Stephanie drove. It had one hundred eighty thousand miles on it and a history of regular, undiagnosable breakdowns. Now Nicole could easily afford to buy her sister a new car. And there were Steph's medical bills, which were considerable. Yes, she thought, that money could be used to help mitigate the fallout from their streak of bad luck.

"By the way, how is Stephanie?" Sue said.

"She's still staying with me, but she's doing a lot better. I finally convinced her to go to a therapist specializing in PTSD. After she was released from the hospital, she was in pretty bad shape emotionally. She kept having nightmares of being buried alive and would end up in bed with me, afraid to be alone. But she's pretty much past that."

"What about her fiancé?"

"David? They're still a couple, but they're not living together, and Steph insisted on putting the engagement on hold. She did a lot of thinking in that basement. She took a long, hard look at her life and decided she wasn't sure she wants the same things David does."

"Like what?"

"The big wedding, for starters. But her main problem was David's resolve to start a family right away. Steph isn't ready. In fact, she doesn't know if she even wants kids. She feels she's been wasting her life being what she calls 'a flake,' although I've always thought of her as a free spirit. She's determined to go back to college and get a degree in graphic design. She's applying to art schools and looking for work she can continue part-time after school starts in the fall. She's completely turning her life around. And she wants to be well on her way before she gets married."

"Good for her!" Sue said. "Maybe something positive came from her terrible experience."

"I think it did." Nicole said. Behind Sue, Hattie Longelle and her companions had gotten up and were starting to file out. One man remained seated to settle the bill before following the others. He and Hattie, who'd been seated together, had been demonstrably affectionate. He was bald and at least twice the actress's age. Nicole recognized him from the news as one of the top agents with CAA. He was probably Hattie's agent, as well as her boyfriend.

That evening, Nicole and Steph had just finished dinner and were thinking about going to a movie when the doorbell rang. Nicole was surprised to see Greg Arnault standing there.

Nicole was so surprised to see him that she stared at him for a very long moment without speaking.

"Are you going to invite me in?" Arnault said. "I'd like to talk to you."

"Sorry," she said. "I wasn't expecting to see you." She opened the door wider and motioned him in.

Just then, Stephanie came in from the kitchen, where she'd just finished doing the dishes, a chore she and Nicole alternated. At the sight of Arnault, Steph tactfully headed toward the hall. "I'll be in my room," she called back.

Nicole led Arnault into the living room. She gestured him toward the couch, while she settled into her favorite overstuffed chair.

After they were seated, she said, "What's up? Is it about the case? Did you catch Ashley?"

"I'm afraid not," he said. "But I'm not here about work. It's because I can't stop thinking about you. I'd like to start seeing you, get to know you better. If you're not interested, just say so, and I'll leave."

She hesitated. She was interested, but she had the feeling that it would end badly, and she didn't need another heartbreak.

There was an awkward silence. Finally, Arnault got up. "Maybe you need time to think about it."

Despite her doubts, Nicole didn't want to him to leave. "I have thought about it," she said quickly. "I'd like to give it a try."

He sat down again. "How about dinner?" he said.

"Tonight? I just had dinner."

"You can have a drink, then, and watch me eat."

"We have leftovers I can heat up and a nice bottle of Malbec I've been saving for a special occasion."

As they smiled at each other, Nicole thought maybe she was wrong. It might work out after all.

# ACKNOWLEDGMENTS

MANY THANKS TO my daughter, Jennifer, son-in-law John, and granddaughters Anabelle and Lila for all the ways they encourage, support, and cheer on my writing endeavors. I also want to thank my husband Bill for his invaluable advice and for reading every one of the many drafts of this book.

Special thanks, too, to my two technical advisors, real-life PI Cathy Watkins, my brother-in-law Jeff, a retired criminal defense attorney, and my sister Susan Scott. They were invaluable in helping me shape the plot of *The Ransom* and keep it true to life.

Thanks, too, to Trish Beall, Helen Betts, and Joyce Brownfield for proofreading this book and weeding out glitches in the plot.